Praise for *Kin: Practically True Stories*

"V Efua Prince's *Kin: Practically True Stories* bursts through the rigid walls of genre in search of the higher truths of family, Black womanhood, and the work of life. Of course it does. Prince knows that such truths can't be properly contained in the rigid containers of convention. They're everywhere, especially in the stories, poetry, drama, and words at the heart of this book."

—Rion Amilcar Scott, author of The World Doesn't Require You: Stories

"Through an autobiographical, hybrid approach to storytelling in the company of Jean Toomer and Claudia Rankine, V Efua Prince challenges genre in *Kin: Practically True Stories* as a means to resist and defy the form of the white-colonizing novel as other African American writers have in the past. Plays and poetic vignettes inhabit this collection as neighbors, as we meet people—sometimes through the speaker's account, other times through their own voice—and discover the textures, complexities, and triumphs of womanhood through an ongoing survival of living in a racist, sexist culture. Just like her grandmother who was a quilter, Prince inherited the gift of sewing together words to show the struggles and survivals of family in the reverberations of history both public and personal while asking, How *does* one love in the aftermath?"

—Dennis Etzel Jr., author of This Removed Utopia

"*Kin: Practically True Stories* evinces the author's skill in balancing homage and improvisation to create a radically innovative reworking of Jean Toomer's 1923 masterpiece, *Cane*. But this is no mere act of unoriginal mimicry; rather Prince's volume successfully recasts Toomer's experimental modernism in order to find its way to a resonant lyricism that is at once evocative of times long past and of places containing bodies close enough to touch one minute and wholly emptied of presence the next. In the end, Prince accomplishes what Toomer's volume sought to achieve: to insist that at the intersection of memory and aspiration lies precarity."

—Herman Beavers, author of Obsidian Blues and The Vernell Poems

T0146123

"In *Kin: Practically True Stories*, V Efua Prince has woven a complex, painful, and powerful tapestry of stories, poetry, theatrical script, song, and journalistic accounts about African American history, presence, and being. The voices in this collection are an upswelling and uprising across the centuries and, like the Furies, demand we listen to their accounts of brutality and violence, of motherhood and fatherhood, of bodies in pain and in healing. Prince has assembled an imaginative, practically true, terribly true, and wondrously true collective. Listen, and listen again."

—Kerry Neville, author of *Remember to Forget Me* and *Necessary Lies*

"Throughout *Kin*, V Efua Prince weaves the story of woman: one who feels, remembers, documents, interrogates, sorts through, and passes on. Appropriately intricate and engagingly variegated, the truths in this collection are always suffused with a core of realness. The strength of Prince's intellectual rigor and the wisdom in the warmth of her words make hers a masterful examination of the complexity of Black American womanhood."

—Sufiya Abdur-Rahman, author of *Heir to the Crescent Moon*

KIN

Made in Michigan Writers Series

GENERAL EDITORS

Michael Delp, Interlochen Center for the Arts
M. L. Liebler, Wayne State University

A complete listing of the books in this series can
be found online at wsupress.wayne.edu.

KIN

Practically True Stories

V EFUA PRINCE

WAYNE STATE UNIVERSITY PRESS
DETROIT

© 2024 by V Efua Prince. All rights reserved. No part of this book may be reproduced without formal permission.

ISBN 9780814351505 (paperback)
ISBN 9780814351512 (e-book)

Library of Congress Control Number: 2024933496

On cover: *Unapologetic* by Imani Bell Prince, 2016, @imanibellmadeit.
Cover design by Kristle Marshall.

Publication of this book was made possible by a generous gift from The Meijer Foundation.

Wayne State University Press rests on Waawiyaataanong, also referred to as Detroit, the ancestral and contemporary homeland of the Three Fires Confederacy. These sovereign lands were granted by the Ojibwe, Odawa, Potawatomi, and Wyandot Nations, in 1807, through the Treaty of Detroit. Wayne State University Press affirms Indigenous sovereignty and honors all tribes with a connection to Detroit. With our Native neighbors, the press works to advance educational equity and promote a better future for the earth and all people.

Wayne State University Press
Leonard N. Simons Building
4809 Woodward Avenue
Detroit, Michigan 48201-1309

Visit us online at wsupress.wayne.edu.

for the children not yet born

They led him t th coast, they led him t th sea, they led him across th ocean an they didnt set him free. The old coast didnt miss him, an th new coast wasnt free, he left the old-coast brother, t give birth t you an me. O Lord, great God Almighty, t give birth t you an me.

—Jean Toomer, *Cane*

Contents

Preface

I assure you that the accounts that follow are true. Pinky promise—although that description does not properly identify the shortest finger on my hand. Browny promise, however, never became a thing. Nevertheless, there is no one on these pages certifying this fact, except the words themselves. Read them and gauge for yourself. You will find them all practically true. Generally, the publishing industry manages this problem of verification by sorting writers into categories. The two large bunches of poetry folk or prose people are shuffled into separate houses before dividing the prose between fiction and nonfiction and the fiction into camps based upon genre. But this collection of writings is not easily sorted. I beg your indulgence.

For want of a better name, I have called this work a collection of stories. The dramas, *Period.* and *Waterbearers*, sit beside an essay, titled "*Amita*," and a short story, "The Family Tree," branches into "June" and "Empty Vessel," hybrid pieces that are difficult to define. The logic of the branching represents my resistance to purely linear and binary thinking. So I compiled this hybrid text by deliberately and shamelessly riffing off the genius of Jean Toomer. In "Lullaby," "Oliver," "Rhobert," "Washer," "Routes," and "Prayer," I have sampled directly from Toomer's *Cane*. Published in 1923, *Cane* gained immediate critical acclaim for Toomer's classically modernist representation of African American life. To understand *Cane*, Darwin Turner insists in the introduction to the 1975 edition, one must understand the author, whose recollections in his unpublished autobiographies took liberties with the facts. Turner states, "In such instances, however, fantasy may prove more important than truth; for Toomer's distortions reflect his own assessment of the significant influences on his life." So too, for me, is the essence of truth herein.

This collection is autobiographical in the way that I, as a black woman scholar a generation removed from Frances Smith Foster, conceive it. Foster asks, "Can Cups Be Books?" in an effort to expand what gets read as literary and autobiographical. Similarly, here, in an age when selfies are ubiquitous and the internet encourages living out loud, I present a more quiet exhibition wherein I embrace literary artifice as a means of revealing a community of people who are alive in some places, broken in others. And rather than lie, like Zora Neale Hurston feels compelled to do in *Dust Tracks on a Road*, in a memoir she never desired to write, I choose a collection of various pieces that have the effect of getting at what matters without demanding an audience of voyeurs. Nevertheless, the collection reflects my family—by blood, law, and choice—their diverse movements and migrations, in their many manifestations.

At the opening, the collection sets the reader atop a perch on a high, thin limb. The subsequent stories trace branches of varying stability back to the sturdy trunk of women who claimed themselves in the face of various forms of oppression. The collection preserves personal and historical stories, which are, for the family, fertile ground. Reading, as Toni Morrison has taught us, is not linear; it is recursive. If the opening becomes more clear after reading through the pages, then the collection compels the reader to start again, mirroring the history of encountering the dark and enigmatic folk who, not too long past, had been classified as chattel.

To the question of why I chose *Cane*, I respond because, like W.E.B. Du Bois's *Souls of Black Folk*, Jean Toomer's *Cane* challenges conventional form in an effort to render an adequate sketch of a people. *Cane* moves geographically, demonstrating the significance of place and migration for African Americans. And Toomer utilizes various genres alternately to present clear and efficient images or to slow down the pace of the work to develop characters or themes. He rejects a black/white binary in favor of a richer exploration of identity rooted in the African American experience. But there is no need to revise *Cane* if I cannot show why and how Toomer's work and my own converge.

When I borrowed directly from *Cane*, I asked myself: Why? What use is it for me to change anything about Toomer's masterpiece in this moment? What is it that using Toomer's phrasing, images, tone, pacing, and the like helps me to say that either he did not already accomplish in the original or that I could not generate on my own? For instance, in "Oliver" I wondered what happens to "Karintha" when the gender is changed from girl to boy. Such a question resonates in society today in ways that it did not at the beginning of the twentieth century when Toomer wrote it. In other cases, such as "Rhobert" and "Prayer," rather than merely echo the original structure, I added my voice in dialogue. This kind of duet allows me to retain Toomer's images while laying my own atop, like a palimpsest, in the hope that the century between us gets acknowledged even as the distinctions appear in relief.

When Frederick Douglass published his *Narrative of the Life of Frederick Douglass* in 1855, the industry as well as the public at large required of him an unvarnished tale. They wished to read an accounting that revealed the harrowing life of one who had been enslaved. Conventions around such stories demanded authentication, which appeared in the form of a letter penned by a reputable white citizen affirming the veracity of the account. Any artifice crafted under these conditions on the part of the author had to be refined to conceal its presence and design. In this way, the story is presented as a mere recounting that only happens to captivate an audience.

An industry, in imposing such demands, is requiring of those African Americans who were writing to camouflage the working of their minds and the finesse of their artistry, in an effort to convince a skeptical white audience of the need to abolish the institution of slavery. The idea being that abolition might be best achieved if Douglass could be perceived as both man and slave—a noble savage. Such a man could elicit sympathies, in part, because the white readership is assured of its inherently superior position vis-à-vis the black speaking subject. Douglass's *Narrative* remains an ideal specimen of a fugitive slave narrative because it fulfills this command, while transgressing it by demonstrating sophisticated aesthetics, perfectly rendering the conundrum of the nineteenth-century African American writer. Their job is to tell the truth of a peculiar experience within the form demanded by those requiring black subordination. Hence, I, being descended from enslaved African Americans, cannot apologize for my writing being neither this nor that. I reject genre as a delimitation.

This matter calls to my mind a memory. I asked for and received as a gift from my then husband a cockatiel, whom I named Rufus. When we brought Rufus home, we hung her cage high with a clear view of the window. She was a beautiful gray-pearl specimen with orange blush cheeks and a pale yellow crown. I became immediately ashamed. For no more reason than my personal amusement, I had put a bird in a cage. I decided that the best I could do under the circumstances was to prop the cage door open so that she could fly freely about the house. Yet still the shame. I had given Rufus free access to the house, but she was a bird to whom God had given the sky.

Detroit, Michigan
Lunar New Year, 2023

BRANCHES

LULLABY

(for Serenity after "Evening Song" from Cane *by Jean Toomer)*

Full moon rising on th shores of my heart,
Lakes an moon an fires,
Loo Leigh tires,
Same day, years apart.

Promise of future ventures stretch t kiss th moon,
Miracle made vesper-keeps
Loo Leigh sleeps,
An I'll be sleeping soon.

Loo Leigh, curled like th drowsy kittens by th corner mart,
Snugly, fetchingly she gleams,
Loo Leigh dreams,
Hand soft upon my heart.

Period.

A PLAY IN ONE ACT

Cast of Characters

ISIS: A still bleeding womb that will never yield, trying to control her life through drinking, smoking, and socializing; mother of one adopted child.

AMAZON: A hysterectomy, a medical violence to counter the violence wrought by disease, trying to control her life through measurements and science; mother of two children.

NEFERTITI: A womb at menopause, having outlived its usefulness, trying to control her life through art and thinking; mother of three children.

Scene

A remote beach house on a Caribbean island.

Time

Following a pandemic.

ACT 1

SETTING: The play is set at a resort in the Caribbean, the kind of place middle-aged African American women go to retreat from their regular lives. They spend their time onstage inside the room, but the ocean is moving just out of view.

AT RISE: The three friends are getting ready to go out into the world on the morning after their arrival. The women are haggard, as if emerging from an extended battle. They are the long-married women.

NEFERTITI

(standing in front of a full-length mirror)

I cant accept this.

AMAZON

Accept what?

NEFERTITI

This. This waistline. I remember when it was twenty-four inches.

ISIS

You were a bean pole. But you still look good.

NEFERTITI

Seems like a million babies ago.

ISIS

You measuring time in babies?

AMAZON

Nefertiti, you cant afford t measure time in babies. You have t pay t raise kids. You are not on welfare!

ISIS

Honestly, Nefertiti! You only have three children. Thats not enough t count much by.

NEFERTITI

(to Isis)

More'n th one you have.

AMAZON

An more than th two that I have.

NEFERTITI

Glad you can acknowledge that. Neither of you wants t have another child.

(*Isis and Amazon make sounds that affirm the truth of Nefertiti's statement.*)

Never mind th one, two, an three. At least a million babies have been born since my waistline was twenty-four inches.

ISIS

(*beginning a familiar story*)

I remember seeing you for th first time. Amazon, you remember.

(*to Nefertiti*)

You were wearing white stirrup pants an a halter top with gold military buttons, except no one in th military ever got t wear a halter top.

AMAZON

Not t mention that gleaming white wrap she had on her head.

ISIS

It was th night before orientation when we were first-year graduate students. We had been invited as new students t th dean's house for cocktails. I was terrified that I would get there an someone would point at me an holler imposter. I was scared that I wasnt smart enough, you know, like someone in admissions had made a mistake letting me in. I thought I'd be th only chocolate chip in a bowl of vanilla ice cream. I kept asking myself why I had even wanted t go t graduate school. Those kinds of thoughts swirling around in my head. Then I get t th dean's place an BOOM! You were th first thing I noticed when I walked in th room.

AMAZON

I was th first t arrive. Isis, you came in later. I watched th room fill with polite nervous people. I fit right in. But Nefertiti floated in with that getup doing th opposite of fitting in! There werent but three black people admitted that year.

(*Amazon points at each of them to count the three.*)

Those white folks didnt bother you. Girl, you were like, "This room belongs t ME!"

ISIS

I know thats th truth! I thought, Who is that woman? I took one look at Nefertiti an said t myself, She an I are going t be friends.

AMAZON

Of course you did! You had t make friends with a woman like that, because if she could turn out a room just by standing in it, who knows what she could do as your enemy!

NEFERTITI

. . .

I saw that outfit in a Spiegel catalog on a model an thought it would look good on me.

. . .

I was a young woman with room t grow into myself.

. . .
. . .

AMAZON

Back then could you imagine fifty?

ISIS

Fifty? Hell no! We were immortal.

AMAZON

Goddesses.

(*Music starts. The women begin to dance the dance of goddesses in honor of their youthful selves. Following the dance, they collapse onto a sofa laughing.*)

NEFERTITI

(*returning to the mirror to continue dressing*)

Fifty might as well have been one hundred. My mama'nem was fifty. I would never be fifty.

ISIS

I am still not fifty.

AMAZON

I know. You're fifty-three!

NEFERTITI

But look at her. Look n like she could still do backflips on th sidelines of a football game.

AMAZON

Thats because Isis's never had a baby.

(*Isis grows cold. Amazon doesn't notice the shift in temperature.*)

You dont know what that does t your body. Isnt that right, Nefertiti? Is your body th same as it was before you had three pregnancies? Isis never had t deal with th stretch marks, varicose veins, swollen feet. I put on twenty-eight pounds with th first pregnancy an thirty-five pounds with th second pregnancy. My blood pressure was elevated. Blood sugar rose.

NEFERTITI

Dont hate on Isis for having th good sense t adopt.

AMAZON

Of course theres nothing wrong with adopting a child. It's very honorable, providing a loving home t a child whose parents arent able t care for him.

An Micah is brilliant, smart, handsome—all th qualities anyone could ever want in a son.

ISIS

(distant)

I might not have carried Micah in my belly, but I have carried him in my heart.

AMAZON

Of course you have! I'm just saying carrying a baby in your heart isnt th same as carrying one in your uterus.

ISIS

(lighting a cigarette)

Whats th difference, Amazon?

AMAZON

Tons. There are like a thousand differences. Look at Nefertiti! An she didnt have ten children. Just three.

. . .

NEFERTITI

. . .
. . .

Who in th world has ten babies these days?

AMAZON

Exactly my point. Women dont get married so young these days. They dont start having children at seventeen like in th olden days. We have birth control.

ISIS

(*taking a drag on her cigarette*)

Praise th Lord.

AMAZON

We dont have so many babies because we grew up with our mothers telling us t keep our legs closed an our head in books. They wanted us t be somebody.

ISIS

I'm somebody regardless of whether my legs are open or closed. Furthermore, my head doesnt have t be in a book t make me somebody.

NEFERTITI

Preach!

ISIS

Nefertiti, you dont need your waistline t be twenty-four inches. You're a woman! Literally every other person is a woman. Used t be that you only had two choices: a woman or a man. You got more choices now.

NEFERTITI

Wait, wait. Gender's not a choice. People are born—

ISIS

(*interrupting Nefertiti and continuing unperturbed*)

Even with all th new options, I'd still choose woman—bleeding womb, swollen titties, hot flashes, an all that shit. I'm a wo_man. W-O-M-A-N.

AMAZON

Say it again!

ISIS

(Isis triumphantly lifts her breasts.)

W-O-M-A-N. I choose woman every time! wouldnt you, Amazon?

*(Displacing Nefertiti at the mirror, admiring herself,
Isis improvises melodramatically to herself.)*

Me, me, me, me, me
I'm tuning up you see
'Cause me is better than you
Could ever be

Me, me, me, me, me
Got just one perspective
I know I know I know
I am th best—an if

You want t know what th rest is
Th rest are my pedestal
t rest my feet upon
While I get my rest on.

Up here on this throne
Out here on my own
Standing out without a doubt
Who dont adore me?

*(Nefertiti joins her performance by playing an air horn.
Amazon also plays along on an invisible instrument.)*

Me, me, me, me, me
I'm tuning up you see
'Cause me is better than you
Could ever be

Me, me, me, me, me
Got just one perspective
I know I know I know
I am th best—an if

You want t know what th rest is
Th rest are my pedestal

T rest my feet upon
While I get my rest on.

Up here on this throne
Out here on my own
Standing out without a doubt
Who dont adore me?

AMAZON

I never met a person who didnt love Isis. Always had th most friends. Not
t mention how popular she was walking on th beach yesterday evening.
Th men couldnt lift their eyes above her breasts.

ISIS

Amazon!

AMAZON

You know it's true.

. . .

NEFERTITI

Seriously! It aint breasts that make a woman. Anyone can buy some of
those.

ISIS

Tell me about it. I have an aunt who kept misplacing hers. She had a nice
set. She was heavy chested, you know. But she got breast cancer when
she was still a young woman. Thirty-three. Had a double mastectomy. She
chose prosthetics rather than reconstructive surgery. They looked really
nice. Natural, you know. But then she had t keep up with those things.
Whenever it was time t go out th house, she'd be running around for an
hour hollering, Anyone seen my titties? She was disorganized.

NEFERTITI

Why does anyone need either of those things?

AMAZON

What things?

NEFERTITI

A prosthesis or reconstructive surgery.

. . .

. . .

They dont erase what happened t her. She had cancer an th doctors cut off her breasts. It saved her life. But she isnt th same as before, is she?

ISIS

She doesnt bother wearing them anymore. Th fake breasts. She's older now, of course. Maybe she misplaced them an doesnt want t buy another pair. Maybe she aint worried what people think about her not having breasts.

NEFERTITI

She should take off her shirt in th summertime when it's too hot for clothes. Walk around bare chested like men do. Shit.

AMAZON

Th police would arrest her.

NEFERTITI

For what? Walking around without breasts? Appearing in public places without nipples?

ISIS

For failing t offer men a place t rest their eyes.

NEFERTITI

For exposing that which society demands goes unseen. You have a right t get sick. You have a right t recover from sickness. You have th right t hide th evidence of your disease.

ISIS

I demand that you hide th evidence of your disease.

. . .

. . .

NEFERTITI

Listen t that ocean.

. . .

AMAZON

It's better than a doctor. I wonder what th life expectancy is for residents here. I bet people live longer just by being close enough t hear th ocean every day. Can you imagine getting t live here?

. . .

(*taking a turn at the mirror, singing a more soulful
version of Irving Berlin's "Lazy"*)

Lazy, I just want t be lazy
I long t be out in th sun, with no work t be done.
Under that awning, they call a sky
Stretching an yawning an let th world go drifting by
I want t peek through th detangled wild woods
Counting sheep, til I sleep, just like a child would.
With a great big valise full of books t read where it's peaceful
While I'm killing time, being lazy.
I want t peek through th detangled wild woods
Counting sheep, til I sleep, just like a child would.
With a great big bulging valise full of books t read where it's peaceful

(*Amazon's phone starts ringing.*)

While I'm killing time, being lazy.

(*Sound of the phone ringing. Isis and Nefertiti check their phones.*)

. . .

(*Amazon answers her phone.*)

Hello.

. . .

No. It's alright, honey. What do you need?

. . .

Th wrong color?

. . .

Can you wear th other one?

. . .
. . .

I didnt mean anything by it. I'm just asking if you have another option.

. . .

I put it in th top left drawer.

. . .

It should be there, honey.

. . .

Well, I dont know what happened t it. Can you ask your father t help you? I'm rather far away right now.

. . .

I'm not trying t blow you off, dear.

. . .

I dont have a tone.

. . .
. . .

What would you like for me t do?

. . .

Maybe your sister has something you can use?

. . .

Screaming at me wont help solve this problem. Particularly since I'm in another country right now.

. . .

I care. It's just—

. . .

I know he doesnt get your style, but if you cant find th one I bought for you, an your sister doesnt have one, you are going t have t ask your daddy t take you t th store.

. . .

I'm sorry you feel that way.

. . .

(to Isis and Nefertiti)

She hung up on me.

(Nefertiti's phone rings. She answers.)

NEFERTITI

Hello.

. . .

Hi kid, whats th matter?

. . .

Your brother did what?! Your sister—

. . .

No. You're absolutely right. They shouldnt have done that. But why are you calling me? wheres your father?

. . .

You dont want t bother your father, who's in th house with you, because he's sleeping.

. . .

You need t wake him up.

. . .

Why do you think it's alright t call me? I cant even get a nap in th house. Y'all calling my name all hours of th night an day. I had t fly t another country just t get some rest an you still calling me.

. . .

I'm not busy!!! Boy, what do you know about it?

. . .

Thats right, I am on vacation. Listen, I'm off duty for three days. You're going t have t wake your father from his nap.

. . .

Nope.

. . .

Still no.

. . .

Not doing it.

. . .

Seriously.

. . .

Tell your brother an your sister too.

. . .

Love you. Bye-bye.

    (*Nefertiti and Amazon look at Isis's phone. It doesn't ring.*)

. . .
. . .

AMAZON

It's th womb. Birth happened an they feel abandoned. So they spend their lives trying t get back there.

. . .

NEFERTITI

Th ancients compared women's bellies t a calabash that held all th stories that ever were an would ever be in th world. They wished they could smash th calabash open t find th secrets it contained.

. . .

AMAZON

Breasts wouldnt be more than a warm pillow if it wasnt for th uterus. Of course, men dont see it that way. Always looking for a big-breasted woman t dance on his lap. Maybe they are recalling their earliest days nursing at their mother's breasts.

ISIS

Thats a disturbing thought.

AMAZON

Really though. Think about th way they obsess over breasts. They be feeming for them like they will starve if they dont get at them.

ISIS

Girl! You are telling th truth! Besides that, I think anyone who has not had t figure out what t do when theres blood running down your legs, your clothes are stained, an you're caught without a sanitary napkin in a public bathroom dont know nothing about being a woman. An essential fact: every woman has had t wash blood out of her panties.

NEFERTITI

You cant say that, Isis. Some women dont bleed.

AMAZON

I dont. I had surgery a year after Angel was born.

. . .
. . .

NEFERTITI

One month I was regular. Th next month nothing. Just called it quits with no advance notice.

ISIS

A riddle: what animal bleeds for a week an doesnt die?

. . .

Every month, without fail. Since I was twelve.

. . .

AMAZON

Oh th not so subtle tricks we came up with: tying a jacket around your waist, putting a wad of toilet paper in your panties, sending up smoke signals t complete strangers asking anyone around for help—as long as she is a woman.

ISIS

Maybe we should elevate a class of midwives t hand out belts based upon th number of cramps someone has endured.

NEFERTITI

Or based upon th number of days her period lasted in a month.

AMAZON

Or for th number of iron supplements she had t take.

ISIS

Th belts can be ranked like credit cards an encrusted with a new jewel or precious stone for each month. September sapphire. October opal. November topaz. An so on. By th time a woman got t be fifty, her belt would have t increase in length t hold all th gems. Th larger her waistline, th more her belt would sparkle.

(*to Nefertiti*)

You wouldnt miss your twenty-four-inch waistline then.

AMAZON

I remember one time I was in th mall shopping with my sister an my daughter. My period came like a tsunami. I rushed t th restroom so fast they thought I had t pee. I called my sister on th phone t tell her what had happened. Of course, I had a pad in my purse, but my clothes were a complete mess. My sister'nem went around finding me a new pair of pants an underwear. I just threw my clothes away. Right there in th mall bathroom.

. . .

I dont miss that.

. . .

NEFERTITI

Every blessed baby who ever breathed air—from Jesus Christ t Charles Manson—a woman pushed out of her womb. Every single goddamn baby. Wouldnt be no man on th moon without his mother! An it's like that shit dont count for nothing.

. . .

. . .

. . .

When I was seven months pregnant with my first child, my husband took me t Mackinac Island. You cant bring cars there, you know. So you have t walk everywhere or ride bicycles. I was young an healthy. Th walking didnt bother me. It was summer, even in Michigan, an th heat was a thing, but it was way up north so I managed alright. A large convention was happening—for doctors, you know. Whole families had come, th doctors an their spouses an their children. They hired my husband t work with th children. Jacob had t keep th kids entertained while their parents did whatever. They gave him a small room in th big hotel where th convention was held. An I slept there with him on a little bed. But we were young. After he had finished his part of th camp for th day, he an I would go out. Find food. Eat fudge. He had Sunday off an Jacob decided that we should ride bicycles. Jacob said it would be fun. I looked at him sideways, of course, I didnt want t get on no bike. I didnt mind all th walking, but a bicycle was a different matter. I carried small, an so I always thought there was something wrong if I called attention t my pregnancy since I saw so many other women whose bellies protruded, an it all seemed so much more difficult for them just by looking at th size of their stomachs, but me here I was seven months pregnant an no one could tell that I was pregnant at all. That was th script that ran constantly through my mind. I remember sitting down in church one Sunday when th congregation was supposed t be standing an feeling shame because there was another pregnant woman in th pew in front of me whose belly was far more pronounced than mine standing there clapping an singing. You know, worshipping God. An here I was sitting. I sat down because I was hurting. I thought she must be hurting too because her belly was so much bigger than mine. I felt like a bitch, you know, for sitting when I should be standing. Like my foremothers were looking at me an shaking their heads because I had so little reverence for th Lord when they worked in th fields. My great-great-grandmother Sarah lived t be a hundred an six, an she worked in th fields th year she died. So even though I didnt want t ride a bike since I was seven months pregnant with my first child, Jacob insisted. He told me that we would get a tandem an I didnt have t do anything but ride. You know how playful he is. So much fun an that smile. We got th bike an went here an there. But I kept feeling pain, like I did sometimes. An Jacob said I couldnt be in a better place in th world since we were right in th middle of a medical convention an there were doctors everywhere you turned. Th contractions started that night, an some spotting. I went t th doctors when we got home an had t finish out th pregnancy on bedrest.

. . .

Spent th next two months lying down.

. . .

(ocean begins to swell)

But that baby held on. She waited an came here healthy. They all did. They all came here healthy.

(continue listening to the ocean)
(Blackout)
END OF PLAY

OLIVER

(after "Karintha" in Cane *by Jean Toomer)*

His skin is like dusk on th southern bayou,
Yo cant you see it, Yo cant you see it,
His skin is like dusk on th southern bayou
. . . When th sun goes down.

Women had always wanted him, this Oliver, even as a kid, Oliver carrying beauty, perfect as dusk when th sun goes down. Old women laughed when holding him tight against their bosoms. Girl cousins danced with him at th cookout when they should have been dancing with someone who wasnt kin. God grant us youth, secretly prayed th old women. Th young women counted t see if they had time enough for him t get old enough t father their babies. This interest of th female, who wishes t possess a maturing thing, could mean no good t him.

Oliver, at twelve, was a wild flash that told th other folks just what it was t live. At sunset, when there was no wind, an th weed-smoke from over by th shop hugged th sidewalk, an you couldnt see more than a few feet in front, his sudden darting past you was a bit of vivid color, like a black bird that flashes in light. With th other children one could hear, some distance off, their feet kicking cans against a wall. Oliver's running was a whir. It had th sound of th dry leaves that sometimes make a spiral in th street. At dusk, during th hush just after th clippers had been put away in th shop, an before any of th men had started leaning an standing around, his voice, ruckus an mirthful, would put one's ears t itching. But no one ever thought t make him stop because of it. He stoned stray cats, an beat his dog, an fought th other children . . . Even th priest, who caught him at mischief, told himself that he was as innocently lovely as a dandelion in November. Already, rumors were following him. Homes in Louisiana are most often built on th shotgun plan. At th back, you cook an eat, in th front you sit, in th middle you sleep, an there love goes on. Oliver had seen or heard, perhaps he had felt his parents loving. One could but imitate one's parents, for t follow them was th way of God. He played "home" with a girl who was not afraid t do his bidding. That started th whole thing. Old women could no longer hold him close against their bosoms. But young women counted faster.

His skin is like dusk,
Yo cant you see it,
His skin is like dusk
When th sun goes down.

Oliver is a man. He who carries beauty, perfect as dusk when th sun goes down. He wont marry. Old women remind him that a few years back they held him close against their bosoms. Oliver smiles, an indulges them when he is in th mood for it. He has contempt for them. Oliver is a man. Young women turn tricks t make him money. Young women go t Houston an run th streets. Young women go away t college. They all want t mortgage his future. These are th young women who thought that all they had t do was t bide time. But Oliver is a man, an he has had many children. One child falling out of a woman lying on a soiled mattress with a needle in her arm. Needle calling like slaves overboard during th Middle Passage . . . A junkyard was nearby. Its pyramid of old tires smoldered. It is a year before one completely burns. Meanwhile, th smoke curls up an hangs odd wraiths about th apartments, curls up, an spreads itself out over th hood . . . Weeks after Oliver returned home th smoke was so heavy you tasted it in water. Someone made a song:

Smoke n hot chimney pipe
Smoke it til you feelin right
Give Buddah my regards.

Oliver is a man. Women do not know that th soul of him was a maturing thing no one could possess. They will bring their bodies; they will die not having found it out . . . Oliver at twenty, carrying beauty, perfect as dusk when th sun goes down. Oliver . . .

His skin is like dusk on th southern bayou,
Yo cant you see it, Yo cant you see it,
His skin is like dusk on th southern bayou
. . . When th sun goes down.

Goes down . . .

JUNE

1

I dreamed I was carrying a dead man on my back. Th stench of his decomposing flesh poisoned each breath. His weight bent my shoulders like a sack filled with cotton. He had been dead long enough for his flesh t yield its contents so I was soiled beneath th mass. But I held his arms an kept a labored pace. When I woke, I buried him without ceremony. I did not mark th date.

2

Whats left? Memory. But where is it lodged? In th brain as images? In th flesh as disease or scar tissue? In th air like a virus? In th soil like seed? In th marrow of bone.

3

It was my baby, all grown up looking like herself but also a lot like me when I was her age. It was she that brought it all back.

No, she didnt do it.

All she did was stretch out an fill in. Legs long as a drag queen's with a switch full of conjure—drawing on her roots in New Orleans. I never let her spend a lot of time with her people down there. New Orleans is just too much. Music at all hours of th day an night. They eat anything that walk, swim, or crawl. They prone t painting their houses in audacious hues. Even th plants wear too many colors. In th yards, leaves lounge in every shade of green with some so bold they line their lips in red an powder on burgundy rouge. Lemon an orange trees sway beside palms. Air so thick down there that nothing bothers t mind. Thats why they always dancing in th streets. A child aint safe in that city. Nevertheless, she's got that city in her roots.

Then, too, her breasts grew way past any size I'm familiar with. Folks always looking at her saying, "Jill Scott." When she open her mouth they expect blue notes t slide out. She looking at them through big, luxurious eyes. Ethiopians walking up t her speaking Amharic an when she shakes her head at them they say, "Where you from?" She says, "Virginia." They say, "Oh. Where your people from?" "New Orleans," she says. "An Maryland." They look confused.

Those arent places t be from.

4

I felt guilty. So when he called me an talked incessantly about whatever he was talking about, I felt compelled t keep th line open. I didnt always listen. Sometimes I put th phone down an did other things. It really didnt matter since he never expected me t say anything. When I got back t th phone, he'd still be talking. He didnt seem t miss me. We had dated for nearly five years—my last years of high school an into college. By th time I broke up with him I was clear that our lives were on different paths. But I felt guilty for turning my attention t other men. For leaving whatever love I had for him on a shelf. He would call long-distance an hold me on th phone for hours at a time, crying, yelling, accusing, pleading.

One morning he showed up at my house. I went t school in Virginia. I lived off-campus an nearly two hundred miles away from him, but there he was. I let him in. My day hadnt started yet so I went t th bathroom an showered. I put on my underclothes, wrapped myself in a towel, an returned t my room where he was waiting. It's been too long now an I dont recall exactly how he approached me or why, but he started tussling with me an tied my wrists up with one of his wifebeaters. Because I lived alone on th first floor of a house, I kept knives an scissors around in th event that a stranger would come into my abode entertaining th thought that I was a victim. In my room, I was never more than a few feet from some kind of sharp object. So when he pushed me onto my bed with my hands bound, I retrieved th blade I kept tucked between my box spring an bed frame an cut myself loose. He became enraged. "You cut my shirt!" Then he picked me up an carried me out into th hallway, opened th front door, an threw me out onto th front porch, locking me out of my house. There I was—humiliated. In my bra an panties locked out of my own house in front of my neighbors an whoever happened by on our active street. I didnt dare make too much noise. I curled up as small as I could an I waited for release.

5

It's always been a mystery to me how men can feel themselves honored by the humiliation of their fellow beings.

—Mahatma Gandhi

6

A group of touts attacked a woman at one of the major bus stations in the capital, Harare [Zimbabwe], and stripped her naked for the "crime" of wearing a miniskirt. She managed to escape after paying a commuter omnibus crew two dollars to hide her from the mob. Police arrested two of the attackers who are still in custody awaiting trial, but the other suspects are still at large.

—Sally Nyakanyanga, "Humiliation: The Latest Form of Gender Violence," in *Africa Renewal*, April 2015

7

Where you from?

Virginia.

8

In 1619 twenty Africans were off-loaded at Old Point Comfort in th area that was t become Fort Monroe in Hampton, Virginia, about forty miles from th British settlement at Jamestown.

9

Sometimes I imagine a woman being coerced into sex with two or three men in public. She is initially reluctant but eventually gives herself over t th pleasure. Th men have broken a trust t take advantage of her. These fantasies always figure white people; I think this is so that I am clear it isnt me. For years I would pray an ask God t heal my mind. I dont bother God with this anymore. Now I think this is memory. I think it has something t do with things that happened when I was a very young child.

10

Virginia. New Orleans. Maryland.

Those arent places t be from.

11

Th boundaries of territory in its earliest formation were vaguely identified, particularly its western limits, an thus Virginia was conceived as extending from "sea t sea."

12

When Europe began carving up th world t serve their royal houses, it justified its aggression using th machinations of binary thinking. Binary thinking conceives of experience in terms of oppositions—such as right or wrong, us or them, up or down—which one imagines as inherent rather than constructed by a society. This vision of th world as essentially oppositional is reflected in European religion, which pictures divinity in terms of good an evil, light an darkness, heaven an hell. Europeans used this conceptual frame t impose order on their experiences. Human experience is chaotic enough with th confounding intrusions of everyday mysteries such as lightning strikes, wolves, th bubonic plague, famine, war, an about a million other things lurking in th shadows t suddenly kill you. But for Europeans living during th sixteenth, seventeenth, eighteenth, an nineteenth centuries, th realm of possibility was undergoing dramatic expansion.

Technological developments were enabling previously unimaginable journeys across th seas. Not only were people going across th water—some of them were coming back. It's no wonder then that Europeans insisted upon a framework that could readily impose order on these widely varied experiences. When th world was flat an th sun revolved around th Earth, things were far less confusing. Folks were saying, "There is nothing out there but death, which is not a problem because I have no need t go there; I am here at th center of all things." An so they found th notion of a round world orbiting th sun touted by that stargazing cleric Nicolaus Copernicus t be entirely perplexing. Copernicus suggested that perceiving aspects of reality required complex calculations that were beyond th average person's frame of reference derived from seeing, tasting, hearing, feeling, an smelling. They were being told that their raw senses could not be trusted (it certainly looks like th sun is circling th world). Copernicus an his erudite lot had science; those operating without th benefit of telescopes an mathematical equations needed *something* that could make sense of it all. Imagine th bewilderment propagated within poor societies by adventurers funded by venture capitalists seeking an untold cache of spices, sugar, an gold that they hoped t extract from exotic an distant lands. Even for those who stayed put, these new notions changed what people hoped for, how they saw themselves, an where they thought they were. But because their frame of reference tended t conceptualize in terms of th binary, these ocean journeys yielded for Europeans a "New World" rather than an expanded worldview.

In fact, th conceptual framework fostered by binary thinking encourages a kind of cognitive dissonance. Human beings make analogical comparisons in order t encode something not yet experienced. We come t understand th new thing by mapping it onto something familiar. In this way conceptual maps are merely a long series of associations between dissimilar things. Th comparison, then, between what th Europeans knew an what they were freshly encountering is quite natural. However, th trouble comes with th insistence that these encounters be mapped in terms of binary oppositions. Binary thinking represented th lands on th other side of th Atlantic as a *world* somehow distinct, somewhere separate an apart from th world Europeans had already known. Rather than a "New World" an an "Old World," there is, for all practical purposes, just one world. Thus, in terms of a concept, "New World" is a bad metaphor that fails t reconcile with basic reality. Still, th idea of it fit for a people who were concerned more with liberating themselves from European constraints than with taking th time t consider th implications of their metaphors.

13

Virginia is a metaphor for th New World.

14

On the thirty-third day after leaving Cadiz I came into the Indian Sea, where I discovered many islands inhabited by numerous people. I took possession of all of them for our most fortunate

King by making public proclamation and unfurling his standard, no one making any resistance.

—Christopher Columbus, 1493

15

When we think of rape we are encouraged t envision it as a problem between individuals. Th reality, however, is much more pernicious. Rape is an ideology. It is a way of thinking about th world an its inhabitants that only belatedly manifests as sexual assault.

16

Knock knock

Who's there?

Me

Me who?

Let me in my house motherfucker

17

According to Michael Doran in his *Atlas of County Boundary Changes in Virginia, 1634–1895*, "Either as an Anglicized modification of a local chieftain's name (Win-gi-na) or in unabashed flattery of the distaff English sovereign, [Sir Walter] Raleigh's lands became known as Virginia."

18

Virginia. Virgin land. No one lives there. A wilderness peopled not but by savages.

19

Knock knock

Who's there?

No one

No one who?

Noonenoonenoonenoone

20

More than 350 years ago, Captain John Smith might have walked th ground beneath th porch I crouched on. Th great captain might have paused on this patch of earth t finger th charter for th Virginia Company given him by th sovereign King James. He might have offered a trifle in exchange for a smile from an Indian child right on this ground. Captain Smith might have had corn grown on this very patch of earth. He might have rested on a log right here on his way t visit Chief Powhatan. He might have squatted here, too, t take aim at an Indian warrior shooting buckshot in defense of his land. He might have taken aim t piss. This might very well have been th actual spot where John Smith himself carved a hole in th dirt wherein he relieved his bowels.

I should erect a monument.

21

There are no heroes.

Villains neither.

22

People do not talk about th horrendous conditions in Europe as an explanation for European colonialism an imperialism. Instead, American schoolchildren are shown pictures of pilgrims seeking religious freedoms. One of th best known of these early settlers is John Winthrop, whose vision of founding a "city upon th hill" is indicative of a kind of binary thinking. Th pilgrim story of a people fleeing religious persecution, intent on building a model society, casts th travelers in th light of a hero. Winthrop draws this image from Matthew 5:14–16 in th New Testament of th Bible, which states, "You are th light of th world. A town built on a hill cannot be hidden. Neither do people light a lamp an put it under a bowl. Instead they put it on its stand, an it gives light t everyone in th house. In th same way, let your light shine before others, that they may see your good deeds an glorify your Father in heaven." By representing their actions in th language of this sacred text, Winthrop associates their actions with that of Jesus Christ—th ultimate Western hero. On th other side of this narrative is th villain.

23

While th pilgrims ultimately settled th Massachusetts Bay Colony, Winthrop set out in 1620 with a charter for Virginia.

24

Rape is not the problem. Rape is a symptom of the problem. And the answer is not to attempt to stop men from raping women, but to categorically change women's values and status in their communities.

—Abigail Disney, cited in "Forging a New Security: Ending Sexual Violence in Conflict," Nobel Women's Initiative, May 2011

25

Th Chinese still grieve over Japanese aggressions during th early parts of World War II, which resulted in what is known as th Rape of Nanjing. Estimates range widely, but official records state that two hundred thousand Chinese were massacred an some twenty thousand t thirty thousand were raped during th Japanese campaign beginning in December 1937. In *Nanjing Requiem*, Chinese American novelist Ha Jin writes about th heroic efforts of an American missionary, Minnie Vautrin, t spare as many young women as she can from th horrors of th Japanese occupation. Western readers love heroes. Creating heroes provides a way t elevate an individual out of her social, cultural, an historical circumstances. It alleviates responsibility for collective action, so long as we can look t heroic action for change. But rape is not really about individuals, especially during times of war. After killing those whom one intends t kill, what is a more effective strategy for dominating a resistant people than rape? Raping a woman—girl, baby, grandmother, great-grandmother—in front of her family an friends is extremely effective at unraveling th fabric of th community. Th sense of shame borne by th women an th sense of failure borne by th men undermine th foundational security needed t stabilize a community. Rape erodes trust. It is psychologically devastating, not t mention th myriad concerns t one's health an physical well-being. An what of th children born of rape? Who will love them an more importantly *how* will they love them—it's not a question of *if* someone will love because th human capacity t love is tremendous. But *how* one loves is another question. What kind of love results in th aftermath of rape?

26

Funny thing: I dont remember how I got off th porch.

27

How one loves in th aftermath of rape is a question that African Americans are still resolving. In th wake of slavery, we have demonstrated th extended capacity t envision th rape of black women at th hands of white men, partly because it reinforces th illusion of white, male power as well as th desirability of black women. More recently, African American women authors like Alice Walker an Ntozake Shange popularized (a terrible but I think accurate characterization) th image of black women victimized at th hands of black men. However, if we are more honest an begin t explore th dynamics of rape an th culture it breeds, then we might see more clearly not just th men who are perpetrators but those who are victims as well. For instance, while rape is largely perpetuated against women, th notion that it is exclusively violent men acting against women is preposterous. Do we have any idea how many men were raped under slavery? When we divest from gender politics enough t explore th dynamics at work, then we might begin t reflect on rape as a kind of disease, rather like rabies, a mortal contagion corrupting th DNA of a society. Then we can explore th ways it appears as a symptom of a pandemic degrading th host as well as its victim.

It's been years since th United Nations Security Council declared rape a war crime, unanimously adopting Resolution 1820, which called for th immediate an complete halt t acts of sexual violence in 2008. Yet on July 6, 2014, th *Guardian* published th article "Turning a Blind Eye t Rape Crimes in th Democratic Republic of th Congo," accusing th prime minister of th Democratic Republic of th Congo, Augustin Matata Ponyo, of refusing t acknowledge that state security services outside of th conflict region, including in th capital of Kinshasa, were using rape as torture. Rape is such an effective means of subduing a people precisely because of th inclination t turn a blind eye. No one wants t see, let alone watch, an act so heinous that it threatens t corrode th very foundation of civilization. Rape has th potential t leave its victims incapacitated an unable t raise a family—there is no more devastating impact of war.

Outside th boundaries of war, rape is more circumspect. Th subject of rape as a military tactic remains taboo, an th United States has been adopting measures t curb sexual assaults within th ranks of its own military. On another front, in April 2014, th White House appointed a task force t curb sexual assaults on college campuses. Rape is all over th news these days. According t a survey reported by th Associated Press on July 9, 2014, two in five (thats 40 percent) colleges/universities have not investigated a single rape in th previous five years. Nevertheless, th White House estimates that one in five women (thats 20 percent) graduates as a victim of sexual assault. An if one in five women, how many young men? An how many are graduating as rapists? Rape should not be built into th cost of education.

28

Funny thing: In 1421, when Admiral Zheng's Ming fleet reached th
Western Hemisphere from China, he did not find Virginia. He wasnt
looking for a New World—an so he did not find one. He encountered
land: fecund—but not vacant. Desirable—but not prone.

RHOBERT

(after "Rhobert" in Cane *by Jean Toomer)*

1

An this motherfucka. I cannot tell it. I know because we are family; living among each other creates intimacies. Family makes its own law. I am bound by blood an law t keep th family, but its jagged edges slice th synapses in my mind. I chase them through th fog in my brain. When I finally gathered th pieces together, what I saw broke my heart an blew my mind. These numbered pieces scattered like dried rose petals as I collapsed, my head hitting hard against th floor. I have not been th same since I arose. But family is still blood an law.

Even now. I am not telling you.

> Who is you
> for me t tell

I am picking up these pieces.

2

Rhobert never crawled, his mama always tells th story. He walked without crawling first an th effort bent his legs. He is th most bowlegged motherfucka I ever saw. It dont help that he wears a house, like a monstrous ol school diver's helmet, on his head. At first I thought it gave him air t breathe while diving. Then you called, yelling into th receiver:
Your husband is a monster!
Well, now thats a bad metaphor, I thought. A man might do monstrous things, but a man is not a monster. It's reductive an eliminates th complexities of his very human existence. Besides which, it assumes your righteous superiority.
Our house is a dead thing that weights him down. He is sinking as a diver would sink if th water be drawn off. He bought th house soon after

I became pregnant with our first baby. It had a snatch-waist of a yard with mice running through it most of th year. Th week after we moved in, Rhobert set th first trap. He had opened th linen closet t get a bath towel, an a mouse leapt upon his head. He dropped th towel, grabbed his car keys, an headed straight t th hardware store.

Rhobert is an upright man, despite th fact that his legs are bowed because as a child he walked too soon. If things were as clear as you suggest, you would not be screaming Your husband is a monster! at me like that. You would have known that he was a motherfucka an you would not feel so betrayed. Rhobert's attractive. Well groomed. Talented an smart. He's got th wife an kids. House with a snatch-waist yard. Look n like E. Franklin Frazier mighta been his great-granddaddy. He made you feel we were together in a special club. But he is a bowlegged motherfucka because as a child he walked too soon with a house like a ol school diver's helmet on his head.

Rhobert does not care. Like most men who wear monstrous helmets, th pressure it exerts is enough t convince him of its practical infinity. An he cares not two cents as t whether or not he will ever see me an our children again. Many times he has seen us drown in his dreams an has kicked about joyously in th park for days after. Here you go telling me that I married a monster like your judgment substitutes for justice.

Did you even tell him that? Did you call him up an yell that at him too? Or just me?

Tell him.

3

I wont tell you what it did t our family when he started fucking our daughter's best friend. It began after he made her into a nude model for a figure drawing class he invented—for our kids t develop their skills he said. Saturday mornings. Free t any an all who desired t attend. Our kids did not wish t attend. She was his best model, his favorite. She, a midnight-skinned, round-faced beauty, held a pose so well. Naturally. He put her on a pedestal an showed others how t render her features with charcoal on paper. Telling me she was like our daughter.

She was troubled, like others among our daughter's friends who grow up fatherless in th city. Drinking. Drugs. A student who had been raped on campus, a fact I learned later from you, but one that she confided in him. An intimacy that you, speaking matter-of-factly, revealed t me because you thought I already knew.

4

Rhobert is an upright man whosa bowlegged motherfucka because as a child he walked too soon. Used t hang with this other motherfucka, a schoolteacher who was looking out for this girl. Helped her with her schoolwork. Took her under his wing.

Took her t th amusement park t ride roller coasters. He liked th way she smiled when th sunshine fell directly on her face, making her close her eyes tightly. He bought her flavored ice an hot dogs an funnel cake. She was a positive influence on his son. Th boy had a crush on her, so much less trouble when th girl was around. Although just a couple of years separated her from his son, she seemed so much older. She had th opposite effect on him. Her fawning admiration made his heart leap.

He felt himself a kid again—not a kid who fumbled for words like he did when he was in school. Not clumsy like his son, tripping over too large feet an lapping at her heels. Not a man-in-waiting whom th girls looked past. He was finally, after long years, a cool kid. His wife never made him feel that way. When they met, she had told him that he was too young. She treated him like that—like he was too young—even after they had that child together an had married.

He never meant t hurt anyone. His parents in their twilight years having t endure th trial. He would not be able t teach his son how t tie a tie. How t shave. How t cut hair. He would not be in th passenger seat when his son took his first spin around th block. He would not be able t buy his son his first condom an give him th talk about how sweet pussy felt an how treacherous. It was too late for him t give his son th talk about cops—move slowly an keep your hands in view—because they had already snatched him out of bed an had th boy face down at gun point when they came t arrest him.

He hurts. Old, deep wounds drive him t th brink, but only in his mind; like his feet pressing th pedals of a stationary bicycle, whirling but never moving on. There he was, moving back into that room in his parents' house after his wife filed for divorce. Back in th place where, when he closed his eyes, sometimes he still smelled his own ass opening. He had tried t close his mind, but minds dont close as easily as eyelids.

He was not like that. He was always gentle, even when it was in her ass. She had such a nice ass. Her titties, too, melons like those of a woman twice her age. That is th way his lawyer described them after seeing th pictures th police recovered from his phone. See, his lawyer knew.

5

Rhobert's house is a dead thing that weights him down. He is sinking as a diver would should th water be drawn off. I dreamed Rhobert was on a bike, racing away from me, th woman he had married. He didnt get far before he fell. A bad fall. He bandaged himself hastily before climbing back on th bike an riding off. He fell again. He rewrapped th blood-soaked bandaging an got on his bike, pedaling as fast as he could. He fell. Up again. I caught him this time before he sped away. Stop, I pleaded. You're hurting yourself. He looked at me. I have t get away, he explained as if I were confused. I woke. Feeling pain. An love.

6

Then, too, there was this other mutherfucka I grew up with. A scroll of unutterable mysteries written in invisible ink wrapped his home like a shroud, while we waited on Jesus t fix it. What happened t him? Shoulders shrug. We do not talk about that. I dont know if Jesus fixed it but he did not die. There were years when he did not appear at family gatherings. An times when he appeared looking like th walking dead. An times when he gathered as if he had not ever gone missing.

Th shadow of his addictions darkened his youth an tainted his college years. His parents watched an waited t see if any of th others of us headed after him down that wayward path. They were not carefree times. He had gone off t an elite liberal arts college an come home with two big cornbread-fed huskers in tow, black nail polish on his toes, an habits he could not break. He decried th injustice of penalizing people for victimless crimes. Victimless says th one who borrowed my car t drive a mile down th road t th 7–11 an couldnt make it home by two days later when it was time for me t return t school. That was many years ago, but that shit hangs on like a bitch bearing pups in th crawlspace of my house.

7

Theres no such thing as a self-made man. Thats a lie America tells young men before they send them off t war. Fight, they say, for democracy. Rhobert was young an could not know it was a lie. He had not lived enough t sort through all th bullshit. It seemed true enough once they taught him t make a proper bed an t spit shine his shoes an fed him well every day that hard work an stamina are all that is required. On his grandfather's farm, though, yield produced by hard work an stamina was tempered by rainfall an late frosts an white folks who could be mean as snakes. They would fix th scales, cook th books, an burn your barn. But Uncle Sam was a different kind of white man, particularly when there was a front line an bombs t be dropped. If Rhobert made it out alive an not addicted t heroin, then he could build a home for himself. Have a wife an kids. Maybe a woman on th side, too, for when shit got too hot at th crib.

Soon people will be looking at him an calling him a strong man. No doubt he is for one who has been walking for too long. Lets give it t him. Lets call him great when th water shall have been all drawn off. Lets build a monument an set it in th ooze where he goes down. A monument of hewn oak, carved in motherfuckas' faces. Lets open our throats, good people, an sing "Deep River" when he goes down.

Brother, Rhobert is sinking.
Lets open our throats, good people,
Lets sing Deep River when he goes down.

ROOTS

WASHER

(after "Reapers" in Cane *by Jean Toomer)*

Black washer with her knuckles raw on steel
Is scrubbing rags. I see her place th heel
Of her hands upon th board, her back bowed,
An start her steady bobbing, dark eyes shrouded.
Black kitten prowls by th base of a tree,
An there, a black snake, startled, starts t flee
His belly surfing th ground. I see th board,
Swollen from all th washings. Bless th Lord.

AMITA

I've always wondered what happens when you don't got a mother.
Without a mother you don't get born. But after birth, what then?

  —Suzan-Lori Parks, *Getting Mother's Body*

1

The trouble I had in graduate school remains the crux of my
academic work: for whom does this work speak? Academics,
particularly those like me who are members of historically under-
represented populations, often purport to write for those who are not
present to speak for themselves—the undiscovered busboys and poets and
the Big Mommas who "finally retired pensionless/from cleaning somebody else's house." What is clear, however, for the initiates into this elite
club of cardholding members is that the doctorate program is a process of
assimilation. To submit to the process is to undergo an indoctrination
of learning to value some languages more than others. Unfortunately, as
Édouard Glissant writes in *Poetics of Relation*, in the academy "one could
get away with: 'I can acknowledge your difference and continue to think
it is harmful to you. I can think that my strength lies in the Voyage (I am
making History) and that your difference is motionless and silent'" (17). I
did not know until I was well underway just what kind of journey I was on.
It is a kind of totalizing process, to borrow from Glissant, which for me
at its best results in a creole, a multilingual, speaking the language of the
academic marketplace as well as her mother tongue. That's why my work
in this field has always been about home. Know that this errantry—my
wandering through the agora—is creole, multivoiced, multilingual, and
purposeful. For I am heading home (if it is still there for me to find it).

In 2000, my single-minded quest for "home" took me to Georgia,
where I was doing research. That's when I met my great-aunt Clydie. I
went to document her oral narrative. My intent was to bring Clydie's narrative into the academic marketplace. I wanted to link my research with
a pedagogical practice drawn from a specific cultural context. Clydie's

narrative seemed to offer me a way of acknowledging the roots of my praxis, which is grounded in an experience outside the authority of traditional academic practice. By choosing to cultivate this link rather than to graft myself to a prescribed academic station, I was actively resisting conventions for teaching and research already set in place. Really, it wasn't much of a choice. Those conventions were so rigid as to feel painfully constricting to me at the time. I was not invited into the culture of exchange with shares equal to my counterparts entering the market at the same time. It seemed imperative that I excavate my experience for its rich cultural heritage if I was to participate in the exchange on more equal footing. My heritage could offer me the intellectual capital academic training had not. So I looked to my mother's aunt Clydie, one of my oldest living relatives, as a means of determining the academic value of how African American women spent their lives.

Clydie spent her life as a domestic worker. She represents the vast majority of black women of her generation who were discouraged from venturing beyond their prescribed positions in the marketplace. In effect, they were encouraged "to stay home." This message was perpetuated by limited employment options and reinforced by the paternalism inherent in the system of segregated education. White philanthropic support following the Civil War led to the establishment of segregated schools, including institutions of higher learning, to train a newly emancipated people to be a productive workforce. Even so, most black girls like Clydie never graduated from high school, and those privileged few who went on to the industrial and normal schools established throughout the South were usually channeled into nursing or teaching. Although the 1954 case *Brown v Board of Education* in Little Rock, Arkansas, effectively sounded the death knell for segregation in America, in 1955 public school teachers in Georgia began signing agreements not to teach in an integrated class. Jasper County schools would not yield to desegregation until 1970, following a court order threatening to suspend federal funding if the state's public schools did not comply with the 1954 ruling.* Of course, all of this occurring well after Clydie had stopped her formal education.

In going "home," I was following the lead of African American writers who drew their subjects out of vernacular experiences. More often than not, that experience entailed disenfranchisement, disinheritance, repudiation, and deprivation enforced by white institutions including the judicial system, churches, schools, and families. Even for an author

---

* United States District Court for the Northern District of Georgia, Atlanta Division, "Civil Action #12972: *United States of America v The State of Georgia; The Georgia State Board of Education,*" December 17, 1969.

publishing her work in the 1950s like Ann Petry, who had no regional ties, the black identity is shaped by the terms established in this harsh southern landscape. Throughout the twentieth century, fiction was used to tell the truth of how black people spent their lives. That is why Charles Chesnutt's *The Marrow of Tradition* shows the picture of a troubling new South at the turn of the twentieth century and draws upon the same terminology as my great-aunt Clydie's story. In both instances, we have a deadly backdrop of mob violence and government disinterest in protecting the rights and human dignity of African Americans along with the failure of historical documents to accurately record events. In her story, Clydie resists these factors. But her story might become a mere parody, a cakewalk rendition of brute power violently enacting its will upon the black community, if not for her ability to pass it from her mouth to mine. Clydie's story emerges, then, as more than linguistic wordplay; it becomes like a ham bone seasoning and enriching my pot—creating community and reinforcing bonds of kinship. And now that I've gotten a bit of flavor, I intend to pass it on.

2

I met my mother's aunt Clydie in Atlanta. Beautiful white hair tucked into pin curls. A pink sponge roller held her bangs. Clydie was eighty-nine years old, a slight, pale gold woman. Her sharp features were worn smooth like a rock in a steady cool stream. At that time she lived in an upstairs apartment in her daughter's home along with her great-grandson. She leaned a bit on a cane, but a lot of the fire that must have characterized her young life was still in her eyes. Clydie announced proudly soon after we arrived that she still drove her car to the grocery store and to church. She told us that she'd drive from Atlanta to Monticello, too, some sixty miles, if she didn't think her daughter would kick her ass. Clearly, this woman who had gaping holes in her short-term memory had no business behind the wheel of a car. But I could imagine that she would be difficult to contain. I loved her immediately.

Although she did not know me and could not recall my mother, she brought us into the living room to sit. Aunt Clydie began to entertain us with stories drawn from her childhood painted in vivid detail. All but blind to the events of the past five minutes, her descriptions of events from sixty or seventy years ago sprung up before her eyes like a moving picture. Aunt Clydie's mother died soon after her birth. She was given away by her maternal grandparents because her father was a white man she never knew. Her telling was so vivid, I would do a disservice to her by veiling her words with mine, so what follows is a transcription of her first-person narrative as she told it to me.

3

When I was brought away from down there with my granddaddy I don't think my mother had been dead but 'bout a week. She died tryin' to birth me, from what this lady told me. I was raised by the people who adopted me. I didn't go under my daddy's name. My brother Loyd was a Darden. Jessie was a Jones; that's my brother. You remember my sister, Callie? She was a Darden. I was a Glover. No, I wasn't no Glover. I don't know what I was. I don't know whether they had me in Darden, Benton, or what. I really don't know.

I was raised by Dennis Glover and his wife, Suzy. They had adopted another little son. My daddy has some other children. Well, he had a daughter— my mother didn't. And he had adopted a son, Rush—which Rush went into Glover too.

These people that raised me, Dennis Glover and his wife, was good friends with my granddaddy, Jeff Benton. They used to fish and rabbit hunt together. He told me after I grew up, he said, "I went down to your granddaddy's house." See? They had been fishing "and heard a little baby cry."

I said, "Yeah."

He asked him whose it was, and Jeff Benton told him that I was his daughter's baby and he didn't want me in his house because a white man was my daddy. That was my granddaddy, now. That was my mama's daddy, and this man that raised me, Dennis Glover, says to him, "What you gonna do 'bout it? You don't want her in your house?"

"No, I don't." That was my real granddaddy, now. "I don't want her in my house."

So Dennis Glover says, "Well, you want to give her away?"

He said, "Yeah, 'cause I don't want her. Her daddy is white and I don't want no half-white chil'ren in my house." You know I hated that old man after that. I never did have no use for him. I didn't 'cause see, I couldn't help it what my mama done.

No, and my daddy told him, "I tell you what, tomorrow me and my wife will be down here to get this baby."

He said he heard this baby back in there crying. My granddaddy told my brother Jesse, "Go on back there and get that hollerin' baby some milk." Jesse brought me outta the room from somewhere and had me a glass of milk and just poured the milk. I'm just hollerin'—choking, strangling, milk just running everywhere.

My daddy said, "Jeff Benton, that ain't right. What's the matter with you?"

"I don't want her in my house."

He said, "Why you don't want her in your house?"

"Her daddy is a white man."

"Who had her? Well, your daughter had the white man, you didn't have him. And she's still your grand!"

"I still don't want her in my house."

Don't you know I didn't have no use for that old man? Noooo, no! You can tell chil'ren things and they don't ever forget it. I never did have no use for him.

My daddy went home and told my foster mother, "I found us a baby."

She said, "What?"

"And we're going to get her tomorrow. She is the prettiest little thing." You see, he knew my grandparents real well.

Mama told him, "Alright," so they went down there and got me.

4

Clydie is my mother's father's half sister. She was raised only a few miles away so she still had contact with her siblings, and on occasion she would spend time with them. Clydie's hatred of Jeff Benton preserved her memory. Since her childhood she knew her grandfather as the man who blamed her for the sins of her biological parents. Rather than care for her, he threw her into the loving arms of her adopted family. Despite the fact that Jeff was responsible for placing her in a caring household, she would never forgive her grandfather.

One explanation for Jeff's strong reaction to the infant Clydie might be that she served as a painful reminder to her grandfather of all that he had lost. Not only had his daughter died following Clydie's birth, but the pregnancy itself is of questionable origins. The line separating consensual sex and rape was little more than the difference between a chuckle and a belly-busting laugh among old boys even for white women at that time. For a poor, uneducated black woman, there was no difference at all. Certainly women knew through experience what Ella, a character in Toni Morrison's *Beloved*, calls "The Lowest Yet"—a white man who satisfied his sexual appetite at the expense of the black woman. Ella feels no attachment to the children born of rape, and she lets them die. If Ella could find no evil worse than the crimes exacted upon her, perhaps a man like Jeff Benton might have held some disdain for a man like "The Lowest Yet" too.

Clydie grew up hating Jeff Benton and believing that he had all but thrown her away. Perhaps he had, but he didn't raise his other grandchildren either. He still had his own unmarried children to care for. He kept only the eldest boys, Willie Gene and Jesse, both teenagers who were useful on a farm, and sent the others to live with relatives and friends. Loyd and Callie lived with their father, Woodie. Clydie, the last of his daughter's children, was raised by Dennis and Suzy Glover as their own child.

The only time Clydie expressed a desire to meet her biological father was when she was nearly a teenager. Before moving north, her father had asked her older brother Jesse if he knew how to find her. According to Jesse, he had a sum of money he wanted to leave with her, but no one volunteered her whereabouts. "Why didn't you tell that white man where I was if he had some money for me?" she asked indignantly. Then she presented a deep, healthy laugh, seasoned with a slightly ribald wit. Clydie's siblings and even her grandfather refused to help her father make the feeble gesture of fulfilling his parental obligation through a one-time cash payment. She had been disinherited from the time of her birth. Bell's death had left her unmothered, and her illegitimacy left her without clear paternity. Consequently, Clydie's very nativity is called into question. Paradoxically, stories such as hers are undeniably born of the American South. While the patriarchal system that has dominated southern society denies any claims Clydie may have to an inheritance as illegitimate, vernacular narrative resists such patriarchal reductions. Despite the fact that she is the quintessential example of "Mama's baby, Papa's maybe," Clydie is far too self-assured to be tragic. It simply never occurs to her that she should not be accepted, and she reserved her most volatile contempt for those who seemed to feel otherwise. This aspect of her personality was evident even as a child. Still, in the later years of her adulthood, Clydie could play back scenes of her childhood that captured her spirit of resistance.

5

We lived in Monticello, Georgia. I was raised down in there, down below Mansfield. Me and [my brother] *Rush went to school. We walked about three miles every morning to school. Rock Springs, I think that was the name of the church where they was havin' the school. And we walked every morning. We had to pass a white school to get to our school. It was down there between Monticello and Mansfield.*

You know, I always did hate white folks.

Listen to this. When I was in the first grade, well, me and Rush both were in the first grade. We had to walk pass they schoolhouse to get to our school. And in the afternoon when they turned us out, by the time we walked down there they would be coming out. And I would jump on me one of them white folks. I'd whoop me one every evening. Rush would have to hold me. I hated white folks. I hated them. Whooooweee! Mama whooped my butt. It didn't do no good. I'd go right back the next day.

We had to take our lunch to school in a lard bucket. I tore up all the buckets she had fightin', beatin' them white chil'ren. She started to fixin' my lunch in a flour sack! I was a sorry rascal.

I was old enough to go to school now. I was about six or seven years old. I know about all that. I said Jesus Christ! I'd whoop them crackers. I'd grab me one and Rush couldn't get me away from 'em. They changed they hours! Them white folks changed they hours so them crackers could be gone on when we came along.

I'd fight every day. I'd jump on one every day. I can remember that well.

6

Barred from attending the same schools as her white counterparts, Clydie displaces her anger onto the children who benefited from the system of injustice. Her daily routs impact more than the children who happen to fall prey to her violence. In response to Clydie's attacks, the white school ends its day early enough to avoid these encounters. This picture of my aunt Clydie, who was a petite woman and who must have been tiny as a girl, bullying enough children to convince school officials to make adjustments rather than to address the actions of an individual child is markedly different than the one we generally imagine in association with the Jim Crow South. It doesn't take a far stretch of the imagination either. In 1915, when Clydie was three years old, Monticello responded ruthlessly to an alleged assault against the sheriff. After resisting arrest, four members of the Barber family, a father, his son, and his two daughters, were taken from the local jail and lynched. The newspaper account reads like a comic book sketch (minus the heroism):

The Monticello News
"The Monticello News Covers Jasper Like the
Sun—Its Rays Shine Into Every Home"

ESTABLISHED IN 1881   MONTICELLO, GEORGIA, FRIDAY, JANUARY 23, 1915   NUMBER 50

FOUR NEGROES LYNCHED BY MOB HERE LAST THURSDAY NIGHT

A terrible sequence to the assault upon Chief of Police, J. P. Williams last Wednesday night, an account of which was carried in these columns last Friday, was the quadruple lynching of members of the Barber family last Thursday night by a mob of unknown parties who overpowered Sheriff James R. Exell in his office and took from that officer the keys to the jail where Dan Barber, his two daughters and one son were incarcerated.

Sheriff Overpowered

Like a clap of thunder from a clear sky a bunch of masked and armed men swooped down upon Sheriff Exell as he sat at work in his office and before that official realized what was happening the keys of the jail were taken from his person and in the twinkling of an eye the mob had swung into a trot to the jail for the prisoners.

A hasty entrance was made at the jail and after taking therefrom Dan Barber and his daughters and son, Ella, Eula and Jesse, the infuriated men hurried the frightened prisoners to a small thicket of pine trees about a half-mile from Monticello on the Hillsboro road where volley after volley of shots informed the citizens of our town that a horrible deed was being committed.

It is needless to say that no one knew from whence the mob came and whither it went after the lynching was over. Men semed [*sic*] to have veritably sprung up from the earth and as quickly vanished again.

A Gruesome Sight

The sun rose the next morning upon a hideous scene—the riddled bodies of the participants in the Wednesday night attack upon Chief Williams. The body of Dan Barber, the father, was dangling from a limb, while those of his daughters and son were piled in a heap at the base of the same tree from which swung the ghastly form of the parent.

Operated "Blind Tiger"

For some time Dan Barber and members of his family had been engaged in the illegal sale of whiskey, in addition to operating a disorderly house, and to this place of perpetual crime the city's chief went on the night before to make a search for "blind tiger liquor." His presence precipitated a general melee and the policeman barely escaped with his life. The timely arrival of Sheriff Exell is the reason he is living today. For some minutes Chief Williams fought and pled with the maddened negroes. Disarmed and prostrated upon the floor with Dan Barber upon his body and Barber's daughters peppering him with every available instrument was the plight of Mr. Williams when Sheriff Exell reached the scene.

Citizens Deplore Dead

When it was known that the negroes had been lynched, our citizens were horrified and their denunciation of the crime was prompt and strong.

Mayor Called Mass Meeting

Early Tuesday morning Mayor E. T. Malone issued the following call for a mass meeting in the court house at 2:30 o'clock: "A mass meeting is hereby called to convene at the court house in Monticello, Georgia, on Tuesday, the 19th day of January, 1915, at 2:30 o'clock, p. m., for the purpose of passing appropriate and suitable resolutions concerning the recent lynching in Monticello. All good citizens of the town and county who deplore this occurrence and condemn this lawlessness are requested to be present."

At the hour named above about 206 representative men of Jasper county and Monticello met in the court room and discussed the situation at length.

The spectacle aroused the attention of the renowned W.E.B. Du Bois who, in the March, 1915 edition of *The Crisis*, surveys the response to the Barber family lynchings reported in newspapers across the country as part of his ongoing campaign to end such acts. Under the scrutiny of a national spotlight, the lynchings became the subject of a number of public resolutions after an inquiry by the governor but no arrests were ever made. And the lynching of the Barber family was not an anomaly. Just a few years later, one of the most heinous racial instances on record is that of John Williams who, hoping to avoid prosecution for peonage, murdered eleven men on his Monticello plantation.* The brutality of these crimes as well as the public absolution of the perpetrators demonstrated the prevailing sentiment in Monticello still held to the tenants of white supremacy. The Monticello, Georgia that my ancestors knew was active participant and silent witness to the blood-letting in this town. While Du Bois heard of Monticello because of these events, my family grew up knowing the living and the dead. For my forebears, these were not poster events for social justice.

Social justice was central to Du Bois's work. He saw himself as the representative voice of African Americans, and Du Bois was deeply troubled

---

* In 1921, under pressure from the federal government, a courthouse in nearby Covington convicted Williams of murder, the first white person convicted of murdering an African American in any southern state since Reconstruction.

by anyone who did not use his public platform to promote race propaganda. This demand that black art be tied to notions of racial uplift was challenged in Du Bois's day by the likes of Zora Neale Hurston, Wallace Thurman, Claude McKay, and Langston Hughes, so I do not confront the same academic realities in my own time. Nevertheless, the divide between those who *live* an experience and those who get to *speak of* the experience may not have been bridged by the social changes of the past century. This divide that had been read onto the body is now read onto the mind and is reinforced by demands of craft and convention. To smooth out the transitions in this essay—making Clydie's voice imperceptible from my voice—would be for me to take possession of Clydie's story rather than to yield to it and to be possessed by it. Her voice flows without colonial intervention like our shared blood through my body. And this work begins always in the body.

In the logic of the Jim Crow South, people can tell just by looking the kind of work for which one is suited. Black people were assigned menial tasks that did not disrupt the illusion of white supremacy. They were taught to work with their hands, feet, legs, and backs to earn a living through serving the white community. As a result, segregation and other factors discouraged black people in general, but especially girls like Clydie, from venturing too far into the marketplace, pushing them, instead, toward the field, the northern factory, or the home. Even as participants in the marketplace, for much of the twentieth century black women tended to be restricted to the kind of domestic work that Clydie labored at for most of her life. She worked on her hands and knees scrubbing floors, standing on her feet before a stove, keeping house for white families in and around Atlanta. This kind of work that involves the body is the impetus for African American vernacular. Spirituals began as sorrowful moaning that masked the defiant will to escape the toils of slavery. Similarly, "the blues," Ralph Ellison explains, "is an impulse to keep the painful details and episodes of a brutal experience alive in one's aching consciousness, to finger its jagged grain, and to transcend it, not by the consolation of philosophy but by squeezing from it a near-tragic, near-comic lyricism" (129). Likewise, Clydie's narrative develops from the bodily experience of growing up black in rural Georgia during the early twentieth century.

The mere fact that Clydie must walk past the school where white children are taught to get to the black school emphasizes the physical realities of segregation. If segregated schools were designed, at least in part, to persuade us that black bodies could be put to better use than pursuing more academic endeavors, then Clydie subverts that notion by attacking white children. Physical violence reminds white people (and perhaps even reassures Clydie) that they have bodies too. In this story,

Clydie Giles in an Atlanta nursing home after the onset of Alzheimer's disease, 2002.

the body becomes a site of resistance as Clydie strikes out against the terms of her oppression. Before she is able to tell her story, Clydie has her body. Her connection to her body is primal, and she uses it at a young age to express her resistance to an unjust system. On the other hand, her narrative is a mature articulation, a recasting of formative moments in her life. Although the vernacular expression grows out of Clydie's bodily experience of her childhood in rural Georgia, it is a considered reflection that helps explain how she makes herself at home within the context of a hostile environment.

7

The last time I visited my aunt Clydie, she was in a nursing home near the campus of Emory University, in the neighborhood where she had preferred as a younger woman to find employment as a housekeeper. After going inside the building, my mother and I had to wait for a nurse to let us through a large door. Clydie lived in the portion of the home designed for those who needed extra safeguards to keep them from wandering off. I didn't expect her to remember us now that her Alzheimer's had progressed to the point that her family found it necessary to move her to this facility, but it was upsetting to see her level of dementia. For most of the conversation she was fairly engaged, still willing to reminisce about her childhood. She allowed me to take a few photographs before informing me that I had taken enough.

Her eyes had grown a little more distant, and she wasn't quite as ready with her laugh. Someone had cut her hair too short to have to worry about rollers. And rather than the feisty old woman I remembered who laughed at her uneven balance while still refusing to use her cane, the beads she wore around her neck made her seem more like a child. The whole time we spoke, Clydie was running a set of keys through the fingers of her left hand. My mother asked, "What do those keys belong to?"

"To my car," Clydie responded. "You know about a week ago someone stole my car. Just took it right out Toots' driveway." Toots is the name she calls her daughter, whom she lived with before moving here.

"Are you planning on going somewhere?" I inquired, although I knew what Clydie was no longer able to conceive—she would not be permitted to wander anywhere on her own. I had found her through my own wanderings at the time when Clydie's travelings along these routes were coming to an end.

"Soon as they bring me my car. My grandson told me they found it. They got it at the house, and they gone bring it over when Toots come. Then I can go where I want," the keys moving furiously around her fingers. We sat for a while, and I asked her if I could take another photograph. Clydie refused. We sat. "You talked to Toots?"

"Yes. That's how we found you. She told us how to get here," my mother responded.

"Toots is coming to take me home today. They gone bring me my car and pack me up and take me home," the keys moving in her hand. Another resident, an elderly man, walked over and mumbled something unintelligible, and I didn't know how to respond. Clydie rocked a bit on the love seat and pushed herself up with her still able knees. She walked closer to him, "What's that?"

He mumbled incoherently. "Look, can't nobody understand you when you talk like that." She turned away with obvious frustration. She gestured toward him, "That's Toots' husband."

"That's not Toots' husband, Aunt Clydie," my mother informed her.

"Yes it is. You don't remember him?"

"Yes, I remember Toots' husband, but that's not him."

"Who is it then?" she asks, the keys working furiously through her fingers. "They coming today to take me home."

Soon after, we said our goodbyes. We walked to the door and waited for a nurse to let us out. The large door opened, we passed through, then it shut with the sound of electronic switches and locks. While I could no longer see them, I knew the car keys were still moving furiously through

Clydie's fingers. They belong to her in a way that this place and every-thing else in it never would—a sign of yesterday's promises. Through the fearsome fog of Alzheimer's Clydie still remembers to hold onto her keys. They have not been stolen, and they remain her best hope of finding her way home. I left her there waiting for her daughter to come and rescue her. Her fingers fighting to keep it all in perspective.

Works Cited

Ellison, Ralph. "Richard Wright's Blues." *The Collected Essays of Ralph Ellison*, 128–44. New York: Modern Library, 2003.
Giles, Clydie Glover Sims. Personal interview. Atlanta, 2000.
Glissant, Edouard. *Poetics of Relation*. Ann Arbor: University of Michigan Press, 1997.
"Lynching: Southern Chivalry." Opinion. *The Crisis*, March 1915, 225–29.

The Family Tree

Th lines of our family story are woven as if by a spider among branches. Invisible except when th threads catch dew in early morning or when they ensnare an unwitting prey. Th telling of it covers much more than it reveals. More often than not, though, th stories never get told. I guess it is too much t say. I learned that when I asked Clydie th Great in what year my grandfather was born. A simple question, but she accused me of stirring up mess. Then she got really concerned about my phone bill. "Long-distance rates is too expensive. We need t get off this phone." Th place where you put th year beside his name in th family Bible remained blank because I never asked anyone else who might know. He died before I was born. Th rest are dead now too.

My great-great-grandfather's gravestone is a thin piece of concrete ornamented with three cat-eye marbles placed in a triangle above a name that had been scratched with a stick while th concrete was still wet—Jeff Fenton. It leaned among many unmarked graves. Th hungry woods swallowing them bit by bit. Like a snake. One day I will take an axe an carve open th belly of th woods t release my people. Those stories do not belong t them. They are my stories t tell. Ashes t ashes. Bullshit. Blood belongs t bone, not wood.

From th way I heard it told, my second great-grandfather took t laundry work like an eel t water. Cho Fang found th small boy lying in th alley behind th Chinese laundry looking like a pile of soiled garments. Cho Fang had them almost in his hands before he noticed them breathing. Cho Fang thought about his own daughter when he lifted Jeff like a rag doll. Jeff curled into Cho Fang's arms an snuggled his face against his chest. He did not awaken. Cho Fang had just moved with his new bride an their newborn baby into a small apartment a couple blocks away. Th gas lamps had been lit for some hours already an his wife would have supper waiting, but he would not go home t them that night. Instead, he brought th boy inside th laundry. Cho Fang gently tucked th boy into th bed, which he had recently vacated, at th back of th laundry. He pulled th stiff-back wooden chair up t th foot of th bed. He felt his uncle Wu Ling's perplexed stares at his back.

"*Xiè jiān r.* Go t bed, Uncle. It's late. We will talk about this in th morning." Cho Fang kept his eyes on th child.

Wu Ling grunted. He had lost his position as head of th family t Cho Fang many moons ago. It comforted him that Cho Fang had become so adept at managing things. Since they left China, th two of them relied on each other. Now Cho Fang had a family of his own, an Wu Ling was uncertain where he fit. He would find out about th boy in th morning. Ling crawled into th bed on th opposite side of th room an extinguished th kerosene lantern. Soon he was snoring. Cho Fang sat upright in th dark. He did not sleep.

Wu Ling awoke happily t th sound of pork crackling in hot oil an th nutty smell of rice. Cho Fang was just finishing preparations for th morning meal when he noticed that his uncle was awake. Cho Fang nodded by way of greeting an went out. Cho Fang hoped that Dora was still asleep, but he could not imagine that she was. Th infant, Ru Shi, would have awakened her twice t nurse in th night, an Dora would be worried because he had not come home. He saw Dora's face hovering behind th glass in th upstairs window. He did not mean t smile. Th smile would irritate her, but Cho Fang saw again how beautiful she was. Bright eyes against skin like th night. He had been compelled t follow her eyes like her people had clawed their way toward th North Star.

When he opened th door, he knew she had been crying. "Dora, come with me. Bring Ru Shi." Dora did not speak. She would go with him anywhere. She did not care what kept him out, he had come home t his family. Th family walked out of th flat, retracing th steps Cho Fang had just taken. When they entered th laundry, Wu Ling was sitting at a small table across from a small child. A coal-black boy who could not be more than six years old. They were eating. Wu Ling using chopsticks an th boy with a spoon. Wu Ling greeted Dora an nodded at Cho Fang.

"Who is this?" Dora asked. Squatting beside him, she asked, "Wheres your mama?"

"Mama an Daddy gone. My sister too." He stopped eating then. His body sank as his face melted in tears. Until th day before Fang found him lying in th alley, Jeff Fenton had been living with his parents, doing his best t care for both of them as their health declined. His sister died first. She had been taken away an buried before his parents began showing any symptoms of illness. Then one morning, his father was too sick t head out t work. It became apparent relatively quickly that his mother was also sick. Too sick t make provisions for their remaining child. "Daddy fell asleep an I couldnt wake him up. Mama whisper like she was telling me a secret for me t go knock on Miss Milley's next door. I was scared. I didnt go. I fell asleep beside Mama in th bed. Th sun came an woke me up. Mama wouldnt wake up. I shook her an called her name. She wouldnt wake up." Dora wasnt sure how long he stayed with his dead parents or what exactly drove him out of th house. Now his small body quaked with sobbing.

Dora wrapped him into her arms. "I know, baby. I know. I am so glad that you found your way here."

After Jeff arrived, Cho Fang never found his uncle asleep when he came in th mornings. By th time he arrived Ling would have rice or broth ready with boiled eggs an vegetables. Sometimes Jeff was still sleeping. Sometimes th two of them would be eating together at th table. Th boy gave Wu Ling new purpose.

When Cho Fang an Dora's daughter, Ru Shi, got t be school age, she encouraged Jeff t go with her. He proved t be as able a student as he had an apprentice. As th years passed, Jeff, Fang, an Ling became like a three-legged stool. Fang had an acute sense of business, Ling was a diligent worker, an Jeff developed a sense of refinement that served their customers well. Jeff learned t use th glossing iron so expertly that he could make muslin shine like linen. Th trick t putting a gloss on fabric worked using th same principles for blackening boots. A boot is dampened with blackening, then th friction of a brush develops th polish. After a shirt was starched an ironed, Jeff moistened it slightly with water, then used th heat an th friction of th glossing iron t bring out th shine. Th gloss on shirt cuffs an collars helped repel dirt so they appeared stiff an clean longer than when housewives washed th shirts at home.

Th starch was th key. Jeff took one ounce of good bought starch an added just enough clear soft water t convert it into a thick paste. He'd knead it well between clean fingers, carefully breaking up every lump an particle. He rubbed it smooth, so that it was entirely free from lumps an of th same consistency throughout. When this had been done, he added nearly a pint of boiling water t th paste. He added a lump of th purest hog's lard t prevent th starch from rolling or sticking an t facilitate th iron running smoothly across th fabric. He found a thimble full of lard t be sufficient. He boiled it for at least an hour. Jeff found that th starch ironed more smoothly an th stiffening property of th starch was better obtained by long boiling. He stirred it frequently t keep it from burning. He added a few drops of bluing t give it a clear cast. T keep dust out, Jeff covered th pot when he was not stirring. He also covered it when he removed it from th fire t prevent a scum from rising. Finally, Jeff strained th starch through muslin or a coarse towel.

Jeff let shirts dry before applying th starch. They came out stiffer by this means. After drying, he dipped th bosom an cuffs into th starch that was as hot as his hand could bear. Then he spread th shirt out smoothly upon a table that Ling placed near th back wall, an Jeff used his hands t work th adhering starch thoroughly into both sides of th linen, at th same time smoothing out th wrinkles. In this way, th cloth took up more of th starch. Of course, th more starch th linen absorbed, th stiffer it came out.

He gave a second starching t collars an cuffs. After starching an rubbing in th starch th same as he did with th shirts, he hung them t dry quickly. Then rather than sprinkle th starch in th usual way, Jeff rolled up th dry collars an cuffs in a wet cloth or blanket an allowed them t remain until th moisture penetrated evenly through them. It was a kind of sweating process like th cigar makers sweat leaf tobacco. Treating th collars an cuffs in this manner, Jeff discovered that they ironed smoothly an turned out exceedingly stiff an could readily be given th enamel-like finish that always distinguished his work as that of a first-class launderer. Techniques like these brought customers into th laundry. While washerwomen tended t work for middle- an upper-class families, th Chinese laundry had been established on th edge of town, where more recent immigrants an working-class people lived. Jeff's propensity for detail offered this district a bit of flare usually reserved for those with higher means.

Many days th men stood for hours. Awaking at six o'clock in th morning an working well past midnight. Washing. Starching. Ironing. This is how th years passed. They lived frugally. Th only time on th calendar one witnessed excesses was during Chinese New Year. Otherwise, Wu Ling saved for his return t China. But with each year that passed, Ling dreamed less an less of return. What was there left for him in China? Here he had a son now in Jeff. Of course, there was his nephew an Dora an Ru Shi. Ru Shi Cho grew into a beautiful young woman, whom Jeff would marry in 1896. Wu Ling drew from his savings t throw them a church wedding. Dora sewed her daughter a lace gown, an Jeff took his bride on a honeymoon in Savannah. Th extended family bought a house at 172 Cleveland Lane, an Wu Ling moved out of th back room of th laundry an Cho Fang an Dora moved out of th room in th flat an Jeff an Ru Shi expanded th family later that year, giving birth t baby Bell.

They had done well for themselves. Atlanta was not New York. There was no Chinatown overflowing with Chinese laundries. Th only competition came in th form of th new steam laundries built by laundrymen seeking their fortunes. Th cold industrial feel of th steam laundry never set right with people, but hotels an restaurants kept them in business, hobbling along. Meanwhile, Cho Fang's laundry found its niche in an unassuming corner of th city an quietly served its customers. Their customers proved steady. Th most palpable tensions came from washerwomen who felt that th laundry had a tendency t undercut pricing. But

Dora effectively mediated between th Washing Society, of which she was an active member, an their family laundry. Th Cho clan had bitten off a piece of th American Dream, which they savored for a time.

Then, on th morning of November 10, 1897, Channing Mutual Trust Insurance, Inc. cancelled its coverage of th Chinese laundry. Once this company dropped th insurance, th laundry was deemed too risky by other insurers. When Cho Fang called upon insurance companies, they inevitably asked if th previous insurance had been cancelled. It did not matter that Channing Mutual Trust gave no justification for cancelling coverage. Nor did it matter that th CFO of Channing Mutual Trust Insurance was Phillip Channing, a primary investor in th flailing steam laundry. Th fact that th previous insurance had been cancelled by th company was enough reason for th others t deny new coverage. It became a loop that hemmed in Cho Fang. Cho Fang came t see that correspondence from November 10 as a kind of scarlet letter. Perhaps what Nathaniel Hawthorne was really talking about wasnt adultery but abrogation. Th insurance companies colluded t drive laundries out of business or t make them operate at such high risk that th owners died from stress an exhaustion. Wealthy landowners compelled th city t create an enforce regulations on uninsured businesses. Th city began leveraging fines. By th summer of 1898, Fang was struggling under mountains of debt. Dora returned t washing t help make ends meet. In 1901, when th fire burned down th laundry, it brought th sense of grief-laden relief that often accompanied th death of a long-suffering loved one.

While Ru Shi endured th destruction of th family's laundry by returning t older rhythms learned from her mother, Dora, her husband, Jeff, withered under th loss. After fire destroyed th laundry, Jeff found work at th sawmill. Th hours were not as grueling as they had been at th laundry, but th mill pulled him away from his family. He had t leave home before sunrise an walk three miles t get t th mill, a trek that he reversed in th evenings. Th conditions were dangerous. Th pay was pittance. Prostitutes t avoid. An some of th orneriest men in th world worked at th mills, so there were fights t contend with in addition t th other drawbacks of his new employment. Worst of all were th bosses. Before th fire, Jeff Fenton was one of th few black men alive in nineteenth-century Georgia who had never experienced work under th hand of a white boss. Brutal, no-count men were put in charge of greater men simply because they were white. They were vampires who sucked blood from others. Th toll it took on Jeff's spirit was immeasurable. He turned t th bottle t dull th homicidal rage that ignited in his chest. He told himself that murder would be too high a price for Ru Shi an Bell t pay. But when he came home one day t discover that a white man had violated his fifteen-year-old daughter, he stopped drinking an started hunting, vowing that if he ever found him, he would take th man's life. He carried that grudge t his grave. After th fire, Jeff Fenton did not live a happy life.

Neither would his daughter. Ru Shi took up most of Dora's duties at th Turners' t lighten her mother's load an t allow Dora time t tutor Bell. Bell was smart as a whip. Uncle Ling taught her how t cast th *I Ching* using a well-worn copy of th book of changes he bought off a traveling merchant. Her grandparents taught her how t raise tomatoes an pole beans, how t tidy a house, how t stew vegetables, how t sew dresses an mend socks, an how t knit sweaters an crochet doilies. Dora hoped that Bell would be admitted t Spelman College. Bell wanted t be a teacher. These are th things they talked about later, after Bell had been buried an th baby given t be cared for by an older couple they knew. It was too painful t discuss th hows an whys surrounding Bell Fenton's death giving birth t th baby who would come t be known as Clydie th Great.

Clydie th Great married a man who moved t Atlanta after growing up in Monticello. Th adage about not being able t keep them down on th farm once they've seen Paris proved true for Roscoe Barber. Atlanta wasnt Paris but still, there was no going back. He raised his daughter in Atlanta. He was determined that his child would never feel compelled t speak in hushed voices when she walked under th shadow of th Family Tree. It was called th Family Tree because of what happened t his family—his sisters, Eula an Ella, his brother Jesse, an his father, Dan—after a mob dragged them out of th jail. That was in 1915, when he was eight years old.

Th Barbers ran some of th best moonshine in Monticello. For years, they had an arrangement with th chief of police, JP Williams. He'd go out t their place once a month t collect a sample of th liquor for th purposes of ensuring public safety. He'd sip a taste while standing in th yard with Mr. Barber, laughing about something or another. Then he'd spit off in one direction an say his "good days" before Mr. Barber handed him a couple bottles t carry away with him. It went that way for years, until Jesse bought himself a car for Christmas. Can you believe that? A car. When JP himself had barely been able t scrape together th nickels t buy his wife a stole, this coon had bought *himself* an automobile in celebration of th Lord Jesus Christ's inauspicious birth. Thats when th chief started thinking about how much profit steady moonshine could bring in with so few places t get good liquor. At first a still out in th woods seemed th right way t keep th vagabonds out of th town square. It lured them away from th more respectable parts of town. But that day a week before Christmas, when Chief Williams pulled up t th Barber place for his monthly safety inspection, he saw several fellas in their overalls covered in dirt from preparing th fields for th coming spring planting season. They looked like farmhands look except their eyes sparkled. He saw admiration in their eyes as they looked at Jesse, who was leaning on his knee with his foot on th running board of a brand-new Model T. Th car looked like it could outrun near 'bout anything on th road. Yet, it appeared that Jesse was paying more mind t th spit shine on his shoes than he was t that spanking new car. Like th car was a pedestal for his shoe.

Jesse was th son of an outlaw. He was an outlaw himself. He had never plowed a full row of nothing. As a boy of ten, JP Williams had picked more cotton than Jesse ever would. Jesse would never amount t anything useful t this town. JP Williams drove th patrol car because he was th chief of police an th car came with th job. But even getting a patrol car was a fight because many in th town found it too luxurious. Nevertheless, he got t drive it wherever he wanted, even if he wanted t drive out a ways t Eatonton or Milledgeville or Conyers, but his name was not on th title. This car here belonged t that boy Jesse. Whats more, Chief Williams knew all of them dull, nappy-headed boys. One of them ran errands for th judge. Th chief had never seen a colored man's eyes, which are naturally dark, shine like that before. Not when looking at him—th chief of police. Not when looking at th Dardens, who owned nearly half of Monticello. Not even when looking at th judge, who had put some of them away for some time. An now, all their eyes were sparkling. That spark lit th dry timber of JP's mind. JP Williams realized that moonshining might not be as harmless as he thought. Th embers smoldered in th chief's head for th next twenty-eight days, so that just after th turn of th new year, at th time he was due for his next inspection, his mind was entirely ablaze.

When th chief got out t th Barber place, Ella was pulling up some tender greens that had managed t survive th early winter an Eula was helping Jesse cart firewood closer t th house.

"How do, Chief?" Mr. Barber greeted as he stepped out of th house.

Usually th chief responded, "I'm'll be alright if your poison dont kill me. You got that taste for me?" Chief Williams would laugh. Mr. Barber never really smiled at th chief, although their talks were full of wry humor. He snorted an chortled an that had t pass as laughter. But this time when Mr. Barber greeted, "How do, Chief?" th chief contorted, "What you ask me a question like that for when you done dragged me all th way out in these woods t see if you poisoning folks?"

Mr. Barber was taken aback. "Beggin' your pardon?"

"I dont have no intention of pardoning you anything, Barber. You know running shine is 'gainst th law." Since its founding as a dry colony in 1733, Georgia had had a complicated relationship with alcohol. But when th state formally passed Prohibition in 1908, thats when th law officially set itself at odds with th moonshiners. Nevertheless, in small-town woods like these, th law an moonshiners often developed an uneasy truce. They made *arrangements* like th one Chief Williams had with Mr. Barber.

"Chief?"

"You's actin' like you's ignorant. You forget that I know you. Been knowing you. Saw you jump buck naked in th creek an eat berries from a bush when we was kids together. You black but you not ignorant." Chief Williams paused t let his words sink in. He wanted Barber t know that he was serious. "How much you raking in by breaking th law like this?" When Mr. Barber didnt answer, JP Williams added, "I want that money." Th chief turned toward th shiny new Ford parked in th shade of a sugar maple tree t th side of th house. "How much a machine like that cost?"

Th mention of th automobile caught Jesse's attention. He stopped with an armload of wood. Eula stopped too. When Mr. Barber pulled a roll of bills out of his front pocket an handed it t th chief without even counting it, JP Williams decided it best t confiscate their inventory as well. "Put all th shine you got made already in th back of your brand-new automobile an drive behind me with it into town." Mr. Barber turned too slowly for th chief's liking. It seemed like he was hesitating. Like he was deciding whether or not t comply with th command. Th chief shoved Mr. Barber—hard—but Mr. Barber was unexpectedly nimble. That was infuriating. Th chief wanted him t fall. He picked up th wooden paddle Mr. Barber used t stir th steaming vat of potato skins an struck him. Once. Again. Four more times before Mr. Barber caught th paddle, snatched it away an wacked JP Williams with it once on th side of his head. It was th first time since they were children that Mr. Barber stared JP straight in th eyes when he spoke.

"Sir, I gave you th money you asked for. I have your monthly sample right here. Since that automobile aint for sale, I dont expect I ought t lead you astray by telling you a price for it." Mr. Barber addressed Ella without taking his eyes off th sheriff. "Ella, get another bottle off th shelf in th shed there an fetch th two I already brought out an put them in th boot of th chief's car."

Th chief's hand had moved t th side of his face almost as soon as th paddle struck him. It remained like a misplaced salute. His mouth moved like a goldfish gulping at food floating on th surface of water. Ella was back an past him. He gulped. She put three bottles in th trunk of th car.

"Wishing you a good afternoon, captain." Mr. Barber's eyes never left th man's face. He held th paddle at his side.

They stared at each other. One in disbelief. Th other with complete certainty. Th chief gulped, "You going ta pay."

"I already paid." Chief Williams reached into th trunk of th car an pulled out one of th bottles of alcohol. He took a big swig of it, then another, then threw th bottle on th ground where it shattered like thin ice atop a frozen lake. He closed th boot, got into th patrol car more hurriedly than he had intended, an pulled off.

As soon as th chief had moved into th shadow of th trees, Jesse dropped th pile of logs in his arms an ran over t his father. Ella also ran over t her paw. Eula was frozen, watching th dust an th stillness of th woods just beyond th clearing of th yard.

"He said you are going t pay, Paw." Tears wet Ella's cheeks.

"What he mean by that?" Jesse asked. "Paw. Paw, what he mean by that?" When Mr. Barber didnt answer, Jesse said, "We got a car, Paw. Lets go. Lets just go."

From his breast pocket Mr. Barber pulled a corncob pipe he had carved many years ago. He often held it between his teeth without ever lighting it. He did that now. "Listen. I'm telling you once, like I told him. I done already paid." A few feet away, Eula melted into a puddle.

Th Family Tree is where they hung them. Th January 23, 1915, edition of th *Monticello News* ran th story:

FOUR NEGROES LYNCHED BY MOB
HERE LAST THURSDAY NIGHT

A terrible sequence to the assault upon Chief of Police, J. P. Williams last Wednesday night, an account of which was carried in these columns last Friday, was the quadruple lynching of members of the Barber family last Thursday night by a mob of unknown parties who overpowered Sheriff James R. Exell in his office and took from that officer the keys to the jail where Dan Barber, his two daughters and one son were incarcerated.

Sheriff Overpowered

Like a clap of thunder from a clear sky a bunch of masked and armed men swooped down upon Sheriff Exell as he sat at work in his office and before that official realized what was happening the keys of the jail were taken from his person and in the twinkling of an eye the mob had swung into a trot to the jail for the prisoners.

A hasty entrance was made at the jail and after taking therefrom Dan Barber and his daughters and son, Ella, Eula and Jesse, the infuriated men hurried the frightened prisoners to a small thicket of pine trees about a half-mile from Monticello on the Hillsboro road where volley after volley of shots informed the citizens of our town that a horrible deed was being committed.

It is needless to say that no one knew from whence the mob came and whither it went after the lynching was over. Men semed [*sic*] to have veritably sprung up from the earth and as quickly vanished again.

That is what folks read in th newspapers. This is what happened.

Mr. Barber knew they would come for him, but he underestimated his children's devotion. He wondered often about th stoutness of his children's spirits since they spent so much time crying after their mother's death. He secretly thought they lacked th resolve necessary t make it in a place as heartless an as passionate as Georgia. Georgia was as fickle as a spurned lover. She'd open her legs an let you fall asleep between them, then set your bed on fire. His children were healers who toted more than their share of other folks' pain. But they surprised him. When JP Williams arrived after sundown that evening, Mr. Barber was willing t go along without a fight. After all, he might even make it out of this thing alive because he had some friends among th Darden clan. In addition t their many legitimate enterprises, th Dardens ran a speakeasy just outside of town an swore th only reason it made so much loot was because of Mr. Barber's shine. He made a special brew just for them, an they were very loyal—t it if not t th man who made it. On th other hand, his children were skeptical. He had struck th chief. Th chief had been envious of Mr. Barber's ease with th Dardens. He had even seen him laugh out loud at some joke Sallie Darden seemed t make for th sole purpose of Dan Barber's amusement. JP had a crush on Sallie since she was a girl but had no chance of ever courting her. For a nigger like Dan Barber t dare t laugh with his mouth open like some coon in front of a woman like Sallie Darden showed JP that he was capable of anything. Thats why he did monthly inspections of his place. Someone needed t keep an eye on him. JP had known Dan Barber all his life.

Left alone in JP Williams's charge, Ella, Eula, an Jesse doubted that their father would make it t a trial. An if he made it t a trial, he would never make it t th chain gang. An he would pay. They knew that when their paw hit th chief in th face with that paddle, his thin ego shattered like th glass bottle of shine he'd thrown on th ground. Chief Williams would try t piece it back together by making good on his invoice. They did not understand what their father meant in claiming th debt already paid. Even if it was, Chief Williams an th like did not believe in fair accounting. Williams would demand he pay again.

Inconsolable, Ella grabbed her father in a tight embrace. His hands were handcuffed behind his back. "Ella, let go," th chief spoke softly at first. "Gal, I'ma take him with me. You let go before I got t bring you along." She held her father in a fierce embrace.

"Ella. I dont owe any one. You grown now." Mr. Barber was right. She was sixteen. Eula eighteen. An Jesse nineteen. "I aint got a single debt left t pay. It's your time now. Y'all ready. You dont need me like you used t, Ella. Let go now." She did not let go. Chief Williams's resolve began t break. He had always been partial t Ella. She was slight, like Jesse. They took after their mother. As a girl Ella played with his daughter Cherry when her mama came t th house t pick up th washing. She took th washing home on Mondays an brought it back cleaned, pressed, an folded on Saturday. His wife, Judy, didnt want anyone else doing their washing. Said she couldnt trust her unmentionables t just any ol' washerwoman. There'd been a string of different washerwomen since, but she trusted Mrs. Barber. Also Mrs. Barber was good with stitching. Sometimes she'd sit awhile on th porch with Judy, darning socks an mending holes his boys had worn in their trousers. Judy cried when Mrs. Barber died, an Judy still mentions some funny thing she told her from time t time.

Chief Williams gently tugged Ella at th waist, thinking of his daughter's playmate running in circles around th crepe myrtle out in th yard. Cherry was about four years old then, more than ten years ago. He had dug up th crepe myrtle about six years back t make space for th extra room they attached t th kitchen at th rear of th house after his brother Buddy moved in with his family. Even before they moved in, his niece bullied Cherry, but Ella soothed her. "Cherry, dont cry. Dont cry, Cherry. Dont worry. I'ma play wit you. I'm your true friend. Always an forever." An later, when his niece chased Cherry out into that muddy creek where she got bit by that water snake, Ella held Cherry until he pried them apart. She was holding her daddy like that now. Still Chief Williams knew his job an his job was t keep order in this town. He was th law in Monticello, an if Mr. Barber could get away with disrespecting him, then every nigger in town would start smelling themselves. It was his fault for letting him get away with so much for so long. He intended t correct that oversight now. An as fond of Ella as he was, she was not going t stand in his way.

"Ella, let him loose now. Gal, I dont want t hurt you." At first Chief Williams tried t pull her away gently. He thought she knew he was th law. Ella resisted. Th chief tugged harder. Mr. Barber stood like a tree. Ella wound herself so tightly around her father that her neck was th only place that th chief could grab hold. He pushed his arm over her shoulder an bent it around her throat. For a moment, th three became one standing, embracing, resisting mound. He tightened.

"I cant breathe," Ella sputtered. She opened her mouth, gasping for air. She tucked her chin into her neck, then, like a cobra, sunk her teeth into his forearm. Suddenly, they were all apart—three individuals instead of one mass.

"You little bitch! You're an animal." Chief Williams slapped Ella. Seeing her sister assaulted by th same man who had assaulted her father earlier in th day tore something loose inside Eula. She grabbed a mason jar from th shelf where they kept th fruits an vegetables they had canned last season. She threw one after another at th chief. He charged at Eula like a bull. But Jesse tackled him before he reached her. With his hands bound, there wasnt much Mr. Barber could do except place himself between th men an his daughters t keep them out of th fray. Jesse had heart, but he was a slight boy of nineteen an Chief Williams was burly an not yet an old man. Moreover, th chief had not come out t th Barber place alone.

If young Roscoe had been at home instead of with his cousins on an adventure searching for toads, way out by th creek, that would have been th end of Dan Barber's line. Neither Jesse, Eula, nor Ella lived long enough t have children of their own. Yet th Family Tree helped hold them in remembrance. As a child, Roscoe walked past th Family Tree on his way t school each day. If he spoke in its shadow, it was only in hushed tones. White people tried t avoid passing th Family Tree altogether. An if they did pass that way, they never spoke. Th tree muted African Americans into reverence, but it demanded silence from those complicit in that horrendous act. Even now, with th terror at th site faded past living memory, passersby have been inexplicably filled with sorrow an often moved t tears. But Roscoe an Clydie th Great's grandchildren never whispered or wept there because their daughter LaVerne, affectionately called Toots, refused t raise us anywhere near that tree.

Waterbearers

A PLAY IN ONE ACT

Waterbearers was streamed as a staged reading on February 20 and 26, 2022, during the COVID-19 pandemic by the National Women's Theatre Festival's Occupy the Stage '22, with the following cast:

DANCER: Maa Darley Bruce-Amanquah
NARRATOR: Destiny Whitaker
SINGER: Leslie Morgan
Director: Robin Carmon Marshall
Technician: Mikki Marvel
Technical Director: Keyanna Alexander
Producers: Johannah Maynard Edwards an Chelsea Russell

Cast of Characters

DANCER: A younger woman
NARRATOR: An older woman
SINGER: A middle-aged woman

Scene

Anywhere in the United States.

Time

The past and the present.

ACT I

SETTING: The play evokes 1881 Atlanta and 2014 Flint but lends itself to any time, any place. White flat sheets hang on a clothesline. There are three hard-back wooden chairs and a clothes basket holding a set of sheets, unfolded as if just out of the dryer.

Music
Original pieces composed by Talitha Gabrielle in order
of appearance: WATERBEARER, PANPIPE SOLO,
RHYTHM SECTION, and FAST FLUTE SOLO.

AT RISE: Three women onstage. NARRATOR stage left. SINGER
stage right. DANCER at center.

DANCER dancing. Music. WATERBEARER

NARRATOR

*(Throughout, numbers appear onstage somewhere highly visible to the
audience. Calling out the numbers is a vocalization of the visible element.)*

number 1

SINGER

fast rivers
flow from
high mountains

NARRATOR

number 2

DANCER

Water has memory.

(Dancer dancing without music)

SINGER

It remembers being in a particular place at a particular time under particular conditions with particular people. It holds onto some part of that
experience an carries it along, picking up new information as it trav-
els. Traveling incessantly like George DeBaptiste's steamship during
slavery times secreting runaways across th Detroit River t Canada.
You know, th Underground Railroad is th precursor t th modern-day
subway train.

DANCER

You dont say!

SINGER

Ask LeRoi Jones. He changed his name t Amiri Baraka, but before that he wrote a play, *Dutchman*, about a black man riding in a subway train who got confused for a moment. He thought he was free an spoke his mind t a white woman.

DANCER

What happened t him?

SINGER

He wound up dead.

DANCER

Oh. Like Emmitt Till.

SINGER

They pulled Emmitt out of th water in Money, Mississippi.

DANCER

Sure did.

SINGER

Water holds quiet confidences.

NARRATOR

(singing)

Deep River, Lord
My home is over Jordan.
Deep River, Lord

I want t cross over into campground.
Oh, dont you want t go
T that gospel feast,
That Promised Land
Where all is peace?
Deep River, Lord
I want t cross over into campground.

. . .

DANCER

River water is an information superhighway. Ocean water is a World Wide Web. A pail of gray water poured into th earth is a message in a bottle sending word, as it soaks into th soil, of th hands that washed shit stains from her great-aunt's gown.

. . .

NARRATOR

number 3

DANCER

Mondays. Laundry begins.

NARRATOR

number 4

DANCER

How t Sort Clothes for Washing

Whats needed: hampers of dirty laundry
                space on th floor

(rhythmic underscoring)

SINGER

When deciding how t separate th wash, pay attention t three primary things: color, texture, an bulk. Dark colors an whites are particularly easy t distinguish. Jeans, sweatpants, jerseys, dark socks, dark undergarments, an dark-colored pullovers go in one pile. Some synthetic fabrics like nylon an polyester are colorfast an do not pose a hazard t other garments regardless of color. Other dark fabrics made from natural materials like cotton tend t bleed an as a result should never be washed along with light-colored garments. Lighter garments can absorb th dye released into th water, an if this happens th change is generally irreversible. So whites that get washed with deep colors often turn pink or look dingy. Colors that are considered darks: black, brown, gray, most greens, most blues, purple, an red.

DANCER

White socks, undershirts, tighty-whities, wifebeaters, T-shirts without large emblems, an white button-downs go into another pile. In my house, th dark pile is generally three times as large as th whites. Colors that are considered whites: white.

NARRATOR

It is more difficult t determine what t put in th load of garments between th darks an th whites. Often these garments are made from lightweight materials that tend t be colorfast. Pajamas, loungewear, T-shirts, shorts, shirts with collars, knitwear, an th like. These are things that you do not want t ruin by washing them with th darks that fade or with th harsh detergents used t clean whites. Colors that are considered neither darks nor whites: less saturated hues, cotton/synthetic blend multicolored tops an bottoms, an pastels—like lemon yellow, light pinks, baby blue, mint green, an soft orange.

DANCER

Bulky items are easy t separate because of their scale, but for th same reason they are a bit tricky t wash. A blanket for a twin-size bed or a throw blanket might be washed along with a few other items, but generally larger blankets need t be washed on their own. Otherwise th machine may become overloaded an unbalanced. An unbalanced machine causes th barrel t spin in a lopsided way. When that happens, th machine will jerk an hop like it's having a seizure until th weight is redistributed more evenly. If you are washing a smaller blanket, be mindful of th color an texture. Blankets often shed. For this reason, I generally wash blankets with similarly colored towels an washcloths. Th dryer is usually sufficient for removing enough of th shedding from towels for it not t be a problem. Besides, blankets an towels make good machine mates because washing towels along with shirts an slacks often raises th nap of th garment, making them look older an more worn.

NARRATOR

Towels should also be sorted according t color—darks, lights, an whites—an can be washed along with like-colored bed linens.

SINGER

Delicate items should be sorted into their own load. This pile should include bras, panties, trouser socks, tights, slips, camisoles, nighties, lingerie, fine knits, an blouses. Most of these fabrics are colorfast, but you should be careful with silk. Despite pretentious labeling that insists on Dry Clean Only or th less pretentious, more laborious Hand Wash, often silk is machine washable. Th trick is t use cold water on a delicate cycle, then t take them immediately from th washer an iron on a cool setting until dry. Afterward, hang on a felt-covered or wooden hanger. Fine knits should also be handled with care. They may fade, so be sure t sort according t color. Also, they should never be washed with anything that has Velcro in order t avoid catching on th knit weave. Likewise, bras should be hooked so as t avoid snagging other items in th wash. Lay knits flat on a porous surface t dry. Be certain t remove stains through handwashing or spot treatment with peroxide or ammonia before putting items into th machine.

(sound of water pouring)

NARRATOR

number 5

SINGER

(sound of water fading)

Th water pours unfiltered down th drain through a hose jammed into a length of PVC piping an angled into th utility sink. Clydie th Great would have considered it sacrosanct. I never saw a bare washing machine hose until after her death. She'd cut th feet off stockings, which she couldnt wear any longer because they had a run in them, an cover th mouth of th hose. At th top she'd twist a taut knot like th ones I'd see sometimes above her knee, put there t keep th stockings from sliding down. Th stockings caught th lint before it disappeared into th plumbing. As a kid I was fascinated by th amount of lint that laundry produced. Th weave trapped th lint while th stocking became a water balloon on th bottom of th sink. Sometimes I'd poke its swollen flesh t watch th water ooze through th pores. As it dried th stocking shriveled an stiffened an became useless after so many loads. Th stocking was an important part of my great-aunt's laundry ritual. But I couldnt wrap my washing machine hose with th foot of a stocking if I wanted t now. Years ago I gave up on pantyhose, so there are never old stockings about th house. Standing there, watching gray water swirl into eddies, I note th absent stocking. Th bare mouth hose spits fibers from my laundry into th world.

(*Dancer's dance begins without music.*)

NARRATOR

number 6

. . .

Do they ebb an flow in th water's slow-hipped drag? Or when th earth an th sun align with th new moon, stretching th arms of th river in a broad embrace, do fibers from my navy blue sweater come t rest among blades of grass? Or are they drawn along timeless currents that have pulled thread for ages from clothes beat on rocks, scrubbed across boards, hung by sailors off th sides of ships?

(*Dance continues. Music. PANPIPE SOLO.*)

. . .

NARRATOR

number 7

. . .

Springtide follows th new an th full moon, when th gravitational pull from th sun an th moon is at its greatest on th earth. Th difference between th water's height an th water's depth is at its greatest range during springtide.

. . .

number 8

SINGER

After slavery. After Reconstruction. In 1881 Atlanta, Georgia, more than three thousand washerwomen organized a strike. Most of them had been enslaved or were th daughters of th enslaved. Some were poor white women who took in wash. Washing was th one luxury many whites afforded themselves—it was time-consuming an laborious an constant. An for these laborers, often th only wage work for which they would be hired. In 1881 Atlanta, more than three thousand washerwomen, most of them black an all of them poor, refused t work until their clients increased their wages.

NARRATOR

number 9

DANCER

Th Washerwoman's Strike

Th laundry ladies' efforts t control th prices for washing are still prevalent an no small amount of talk is occasioned thereby. Th women have a thoroughly organized association an additions t th membership are being made each day. In th association there is a committee denominated th visiting committee, an th duties of this few is implied in assemble at a designated place early in th morning, an after a consultation divide an spread themselves over th city. During th day th house of every colored woman who is not a member of th association is visited an a regular siege begun, an in nearly every instance an addition t th membership is th result. In this way th meetings, which are had every night, are largely attended an generally very demonstrative. Th body has a regular corps of officers an th conventions are up t style. Speeches advocating their rights an exhorting th members t remain firm are numerous an frequent. T several families whose washing left home Monday morning th clothing has been returned ringing wet, th woman having become a member of th association after taking th washing away. It is rumored that house help is also on th eve of a strike.

—*Atlanta Constitution,* July 21, 1881

NARRATOR

number 10

(*Singer steps up on a chair like a soapbox.*)

SINGER

T th citizens of Atlanta

It is well known, an has been for years, that th washerwomen of Atlanta receive less compensation for their labors than was paid for similar labor anywhere else, an far less than was paid here for other similar services.

More than twelve months since, at th suggestion of Mrs. Askew, from Rome, th Washerwoman's Association was organized an now numbers over eight hundred members.

Much care an attention has been devoted t ascertaining th prices an rules that prevail for washing in other localities, an th association has finally agreed upon a schedule of prices for service, which will average from ten t twenty percent less than is charged for th same services t other localities. We are not unmindful of th fact that even this change from th practice so long in vogue will t some extent change th domestic service of th city.

But th citizens may rest assured that while th association intends t protect their rights, they do not intend in any single instance t demand more, an earnestly request th citizens t examine our schedule of prices herewith, an consider th labor t be performed before condemning our action.

(*Narrator steps up on another chair like a soapbox.*)

NARRATOR

Price List   Washerwomen's Association of Atlanta. Family washing, including fancy dresses, etc., per dozen

SINGER

one dollar

NARRATOR

family washing, excluding fancy fluted dresses for ladies an children; starched clothes per dozen

DANCER

one dollar

NARRATOR

for rough dried clothes per dozen

DANCER

fifteen t twenty-five cents

NARRATOR

Th following price for each separate article:

SINGER

blankets, fifty cents per pair; bed quilts, twenty-five cents

DANCER

bibs, two cents; boys' shirts, eight t ten cents; bonnets, twenty-five cents; corsets, ten cents; children's plain dresses, ten cents; children's dresses fancy, twenty-five cents t one dollar

SINGER

coats, fifteen cents t fifty cents; drawers, six cents

(Narrator hops down from chair soapbox.)

NARRATOR

plain dresses, fifteen cents

SINGER

fancy dresses, twenty-five cents t two dollars

DANCER

nightgowns, ten cents t one dollar

SINGER

handkerchiefs, two an a half cents

NARRATOR

napkins, three cents

DANCER

pants, twenty t fifty cents

SINGER

pillowcases, five cents

NARRATOR

flannel skirts, fifteen t twenty cents

DANCER

stockings, five cents per pair

SINGER

socks, five cents per pair

NARRATOR

tablecloths, ten t fifty cents; towels, four cents; vests, fifteen t twenty-five cents

(*Dancer steps up on chair soapbox to introduce herself.*)

DANCER

Savannah Carter, president

(*Singer steps up on chair soapbox to introduce herself.*)

SINGER

Mrs. Askew, vice president

NARRATOR

TH NEW STEAM LAUNDRY. "It Is an Ill Wind That Blows No Good."

Th washerwomen of Atlanta having "struck" for very unreasonably high prices, a number of our most substantial citizens have quietly gone t work t make up a large cash capital, an will at an early day (as th stock is nearly all subscribed already) start an extensive Steam Laundry. Th capacity of a new laundry will be equal t th wants of th whole city, an everything will be done on th latest an most approved methods. Clothes sent t th laundry in th morning will be returned t th owners in th evening of th same day. From fifty t one hundred smart Yankee girls experienced in th business, will be employed in running it an th calculation of those having th enterprise in hand, is that at th very moderate charge, say an average of twenty, t thirty cents per dozen th profits will be sufficient t give all th stock holders fair dividends an their washing besides. We are glad t chronicle this movement. It will be a great boom t housekeepers in more ways than one.

—*Atlanta Constitution*, July 24, 1881

. . .

(*IMAGE projected onto the sheets hanging on the clothesline.*)

AVOID
THIS NEEDLESS
RISK

**OUR WAY SAFE-
GUARDS YOUR
HEALTH AND
YOUR CLOTHES**

Washing sent out to a washerwoman's home is often
exposed to conditions fraught with danger for you and
your children. Avoid this risk--send your clothes to
our laundry and assure yourself that they will be done
under the most sanitary conditions. We invite you to
come and see for yourself.

PHONE FOR SERVICE TODAY

CLASSY CLEANERS
SHEPHERD
**LAUNDRIES
CO.**

315 SOUTH ALAMO   CROCKETT 2813

(Dancer and Singer hop down from chair soapbox.)

NARRATOR

number 11

DANCER

Why did they take th risk?

SINGER

Th money. Trying t cut costs, officials switched th city's water supply on
April 25, 2014, t th Flint River without first putting th proper protections
in place.

DANCER

Folks knew immediately something wasnt right, but th city told everyone
t just relax.

NARRATOR

Relax! Our way safeguards your wealth an your health. Theres no danger t you or your children.

(*Narrator leans in as if listening to someone in the crowd.*)

Th tests done by th university? Dont worry about those tests. People looking for lead find it—because thats what they're looking for. Water in older cities like ours is often exposed t conditions that produce negative test results. Flint does not need academic participation that merely fans political flames. It's irresponsible!

SINGER

Lead literally pouring into th city.

DANCER

You cant trust th water flowing out of your own tap.

NARRATOR

number 12

DANCER an SINGER

Water remembers where it's been.

(*Dancer dancing. Music. RHYTHM SECTION.*)

NARRATOR

number 13

(*rhythmic underscoring*)

. . .

Hydrologic cycle—th continuous movement of water over millions of years in forms including rain, ice melt, volcanic steam, fog, evaporation, underground rivers, snow, clouds, ice caps, glaciers, an th like, on, through, above, an below th earth's surface.

. . .

(Dancer dancing)

number 14

DANCER an SINGER

Like water, th line of women washing remains unbroken.

NARRATOR

number 15

DANCER

I brought my first washing machine two weeks after my daughter was born. She was born on April 14, 2014, in Ann Arbor. I was just finishing school. We moved t Flint as soon as we got home from th hospital. It wasnt a hard move because we didnt own much of anything. All of it fit in th back of a pickup truck. Some clothes, an old couch a friend was about t throw away. A small table. A futon. A couple of chairs. A few dishes. We had a black, iron skillet an a coffeepot Mama used whenever she came from Atlanta t visit.

Before we had even unpacked, I went t Sears an spent four hundred an fifty dollars for a Kenmore washer. How could I not? It was so necessary. Or it was a luxury for which I was willing t sacrifice. Cloth diapers required steaming hot water, bleach, Ivory Snow, an a clean machine.

Before th baby, I'd stuff laundry bags an baskets full of dirty clothes an cart them off t th laundromat. Th laundromat had rows of industrial-size washers an dryers. Th washers ran for a dollar fifty an th dryer cost one dollar. One machine held twice as much laundry—if you had a load that large. Th real wonder of a laundromat was that I could occupy several machines at once. There was a rhythm t it, a choreography. Laundromats have metal baskets with tall poles t keep them from being stolen an wheels that turned easily in any direction. They were th right height t saddle up t one of those broad front loaders. Mounds of damp wet items had t be sorted through before deciding on how they should dry. Some items required special care—lay flat t dry or fold over a hanger. Most would be tossed into a machine t dry at high heat after checking t be sure that it was free of debris like a peppermint candy or a stray ink pen.

Then, too, there were tables. Baskets of freshly dried clothes wheeled over t an ample table could be folded before they were prepared for transport. Shirts could be buttoned at th collar, th second button, th sixth an th last. Then turned front down an th sleeves straightened along th seam. Th shoulders turned toward th middle of th back, so that th sides align with th collar edges. Th sleeves fold over, then th tail of th shirt folded up, into th bodice. I like t fold it once more, so that when th front of th shirt is placed face up, th collar appears as belle of th ball. An jeans, same thing. On those tables they can be laid out before folding them in half lengthwise—th crotch seam pulled from th back t th front. After lining up th seams, fold them in half about at th knee an then in half again. You wash it an dry it, these tables can handle piles of anything.

But somehow, I couldnt trust them with my brand-new baby's onesies. Towels, tablecloths, blankets, clothes, linens, underwear, T-shirts. But th newborn onesies. No. Anything but that.

(*Dancer dancing. Music. PANPIPE SOLO.*)

NARRATOR

number 16

. . .

Neap tide follows th first-quarter an th third-quarter moon, when th gravitational pull from th sun an th moon is at its least on th earth. Th difference between th water's height an th water's depth is at its minimum range during neap tide. Neap means without th power.

. . .

number 17

DANCER

When I was about six years old, I kept going into th linen closet t get sheets an blankets t play with. I had no appreciation for th time my mother spent caring for those shelves of clean an neatly folded linens placed there in order for them t be fresh for our beds. I only cared about th things of my own creation. My room was a world—Dunkeygawl. Dunkeygawl was peopled by a royal family who ruled with their legion of daughters. I sectioned th floor into real estate, plots allotted t particular families. These families were elaborate groupings of stuffed animals, which were sorted according t a logic my mother could not discern. I placed a gray long-eared rabbit wearing a large white ribbon, a brown bear in a green knit skullcap an matching scarf, a large yellow-footed frog, an a crisp, white cat in one grouping; in another I'd sort a brown jackrabbit, along with a brown bear with a dark leather nose, a fat white bear with a blue scarf, a white carousal horse draped in pink flowers, an a little brown-skinned girl riding a tricycle in a snow globe. Across th room on th floor in front of a window, there'd be a white bear with red an white polka-dot inner ears an a red heart-shaped nose that looked just like one I had on th other side of Dunkeygawl in another family of two more bears—one tiny, with brown an white gingham feet, an th other a bit larger wearing tan corduroy pants, a tweed vest, an a bow tie—an a giant pink pig with a purple-striped belly that squealed if you hugged it. It may have appeared that th kingdom of Dunkeygawl had no order apart from th groupings. But try t move one member of a family across town. Th people of Dunkeygawl were clear about who was whom an t whose family they belonged. An at some point, we decided that sheets were essential t our nation.

Sheets draped from th headboard formed peaks an valleys across t th bookshelf an over th back of a chair. They bent window light into new hues. They cast shadows that gave th land of Dunkeygawl an air of naive mystery. Sheets were, in fact, essential—how else could a place like Dunkeygawl be? However, my mother did not believe in th magic of sheets t make a world from a little girl's room. Instead, she saw a fair amount of work being undone. A day's worth of washing, drying, sometimes ironing, always folding, handled frivolously. In response, she set out t establish clear rules. She gave me permission t use th blanket from my bed, but she forbad me t pull clean sheets from th shelves. So th day following these new directives, when she discovered a sheet, still half-folded, in my room on th floor my mother confronted me.

SINGER

"Where did this sheet come from?"

DANCER

"Off my bed."

SINGER

"Honey, this sheet right here?"

(*Singer points at an imaginary sheet on the floor.*)

DANCER

"Umm hmm."

SINGER

"Where did you get it?"

DANCER

"From my bed."

SINGER

"You are telling me that this sheet was on your bed?"

DANCER

"Umm hmm."

SINGER

"Really? Thats where this sheet came from today? You pulled this sheet off your bed?"

DANCER

"You tolllle me not ta take one outta th clossseeett."

SINGER

"Thats right. So you didnt take this sheet right here on th floor in front of you from th closet this morning?"

DANCER

"Uh mmmm."

SINGER

"Thats a 'no'?"

(*Dancer shakes her head passionately.*)

SINGER

"Well, who folded that sheet then?"

DANCER

(*aside*)

Damn.

. . .

"I did."

. . .

SINGER

"You folded this sheet like that?"

DANCER

"Umm hmmm."

. . .

(*Singer picks up the imaginary sheet. Shakes it into drapery.*)

SINGER

"Do it again."

. . .

I have t give it t her. She went about th work with a seriousness that spoke well of th strong work ethic from which she came. She bent an pulled th sheet out until it covered th entire kingdom of Dunkeygawl. She crawled from corner t corner, tugging this way, pulling that way, dragging here an then there. She went on intently figuring how th magic of folding had been worked. Conjuring with all her will. She never admitted defeat. Th task was a setup, of course. It could not be done. Folding was a signature. There isnt another person in th household who could turn a flat sheet into a bundle as tight as I.

. . .

"Stop. Just stop. Get up an give me that sheet."

. . .

"It will take you another twenty years t fold a sheet like that."

. . .

NARRATOR

number 18

SINGER

How t Fold a Set of Sheets
Whats needed: a freshly laundered set of sheets

*(Dancer picks up the laundry basket and attempts to follow
the instructions with increasing frustration for
herself and humor for the audience.)*

SINGER

Begin with th fitted sheet. Turn th sheet inside out so that th seams are visible. Grab th sheet at th point where th seam ends t form one corner an allow th sides t fall inward toward th middle. While holding this corner seam in one hand, grab th seam on th parallel side so that you are holding two corner points. As much as possible, create a smooth fold where th fabric for th side panel falls toward th center of th sheet. Th elastic may make this process difficult. Bring th two corners together, then tuck one corner inside th other; flipping th outer one right side out, align th end points of th seams. Repeat th process of tucking one corner inside th other, turning th outer corner right side out, an aligning th end points of th seams. Encourage th elastic edges t fall toward th center of th sheet. Align th folds until they are as square as possible. Bring th corners together an run your free hand along th edge until it meets th fold. Pull th fold taught. Repeat this process, smoothing th sheet as much as possible between folds. Once th sheet is th length of a shelf in th linen closet, fold th sheet in threes from th opposite direction.

Th flat sheet is easier t fold than th fitted sheet. Begin by identifying th head of th sheet. It generally has a border, while th foot usually has a hem. Bring a head corner together with a foot corner, aligning them as perfectly as possible. Rotate th sheet so that you hold two matched corners in one hand an a folded corner in th other. Shake th sheet t encourage th sheet t fall into a straight fold. Bring th folded corner t meet th two corners. Run your finger along th edge of th sheets, pulling at each layer until they meet as neatly as possible. Sometimes th seams are deeply wrinkled an need firm correction. When you get t th fold, pull taught. Bring one corner t meet th other corner. Hold firmly an shake t encourage th fold. Repeat th process until th sheet is th length of a shelf in th linen closet, then fold th sheet in threes from th opposite direction.

Hold one pillowcase at th sewn side by th corners an shake with a firm pop. Bring th two corners together. Fold th pillowcase in half, bringing th seam t meet th open end. Fold th pillowcase in thirds. Place th folded pillowcase on top of th folded flat sheet an th flat sheet on top of th folded fitted sheet. Put all three inside th remaining pillowcase. Fold th open end underneath an store in th linen closet.

NARRATOR

number 19

SINGER

Plenty of sheets but hardly a single towel or blanket in th linen closet. Seems like every time th kids take a shower they grab a fresh towel. I cant tell if they forget t carry th towel t th bathroom or if they actually like a clean towel. It doesnt matter how many times I say,

NARRATOR

"Aint no maid living in this house"

SINGER

or, more gently,

NARRATOR

"Please dont grab a clean towel every time you bathe."

SINGER

On th way t th bathroom they are going t get a new towel. They use them once, then throw them on th floor like they're living at th Holiday Inn.

I half expect t come home one day an find a peephole carved in their doors an a Do Not Disturb sign hanging from th knob. They'll expect me t knock an yell,

NARRATOR

"HOUSEKEEPING"

SINGER

before opening th door. Their rooms are littered with barely used towels an overused socks an sweatshirts they've somehow acquired from friends. Teenagers may not let you in; they'll shut their doors an text at dinner. But they throw their dirty clothes on th floor an let their hampers overflow. Laundry is an invitation t enter your kid's room, t look under their beds, t rifle through their pockets, t open their drawers, t go into th closets, an, like GPS, t track where they've been.

NARRATOR

number 20

SINGER

Water remembers.

DANCER

Laundry forgets.

NARRATOR

number 21

TH DOUGHTY WASHERWOMEN
Holding Out for an Advance in Wages

Th Washerwomen's strike is assuming vast proportions an despite th apparent independence of th white people, is causing quite an inconvenience among our citizens.

In one instance th demand for one dollar per dozen was acceded t. Those who decline t give this price are still wanting washers. Several families who have declined t pay th price demanded, have determined t send their clothing t Marietta where they have secured laundry service. Th strikers hold daily meetings an are exhorted by th leaders, who are confident that th demands will be granted. Th committees still visit th women an induce them t join th strike an when a refusal is met threats of personal violence are freely indulged in t such an extent as t cause a compromise with their demands. There are some families in Atlanta who have been unable t have any washing done for more than two weeks.

Not only th washerwomen, but th cooks, house servants an nurses are asking increases. Th combinations are being managed by th laundry ladies.

—*Atlanta Constitution*, July 26, 1881

. . .

number 22

SINGER

After Great-Granddaddy Roscoe died, Clydie th Great moved into an apartment above my aunt Queen's Atlanta home. But for th better part of th twentieth century, she had lived with Great-Granddaddy in Conyers, Georgia. While her children were school age, Clydie th Great took in laundry. After th kids got grown an married, Clydie th Great bought herself a Ford an drove thirty miles from Conyers t Avondale or Emory every weekday t work. She earned her living dusting, sweeping, mopping, waxing floors, scrubbing toilets, cleaning windows, washing dishes, scouring th stove an oven, making beds, an doing laundry—washing, drying, folding, an ironing. Years later, she'd sit me down, laughing a laugh too stout for her small frame, an she'd tell me how it had been for her.

DANCER

Clydie th Great:

NARRATOR

I was a mess. But thats alright I took care a me. I worked. Oh yeah, I worked. I didnt like public work. I had one public job in my life an I said then I would never work public again. Uooo, Lawd. It was out on Richard Street. Puttin' papers together or books like this, you know. It was some paperwork. I got mad with th head lady an cursed her ass out an left out from there. I didnt do no more public work. I went t private homes, day work. Some white people I would work maybe a day a week, some two days, all around in Avondale an Decatur, all out in Emory.

I likeded that private home working. 'Cause most of them that I worked for, they worked. Werent nobody there but me an I could go in there in th mornin' an do what I had t do. Wash, clean up, iron—do what they were supposed t be doin', I had t do it, you know. An if they had any children, if th little children couldnt go t school, I had t take care of them. I worked for a family, th Lesters, more days straight. I'd have one day in Avondale or Decatur or wherever, but you made good money doin' that. I made better money doin' that than tryin' t do somethin' else, you know. Better'n when I was takin' in wash.

Let me tell you somethin' funny. A friend of mine got me a day job out from Avondale about two do's down from where she was workin'. Around about when lunchtime come, that damn white woman, she got a little dog. She had a back porch fenced in an th dog was out on th back porch. She fixed a lunch an put it on a plate an set it out on th back porch where th dog was for me t eat. She say,

SINGER

"Clydie, your lunch out there."

DANCER

"Where?"

SINGER

"Out there on th back porch."

DANCER

(*aside*)

"Out on that porch? Is you losin' your mind?"

NARRATOR

I went on out there an she had it sittin' up on somethin'. An that little ol' dog was out there yappin'. I turned around an went back in there an said,

DANCER

"Would you give me my money please? I dont eat with dogs."

NARRATOR

I said,

DANCER

"I didnt come over here t see about no dogs. I came over here t clean up this house. I done cleaned up th house so you pay me an' let me get th hell away from here."

NARRATOR

She paid me an I left that food. I didnt eat. She gone feed me with th dog out there on th porch. I said,

DANCER

"Ohhh, nooo."

NARRATOR

An that friend of mine, she got me that day an I told her what happened an she said,

SINGER

"Clyde, you aint goin' back?"

DANCER

"No."

SINGER

"Well, I cant blame you. I never heard of such."

NARRATOR

Those white people used t do some stuff t us niggers, oh yeah. There were mighty few who wouldnt. You would be lucky t find a good person t work for. Th Lesters were good an they had two sons. Her baby boy was scared of me. I reckon that he aint never seen no niggers before. He was walkin'—about a year old or so. He wouldnt let me get near him. His mama would tell me what t fix for his lunch or whatever an honey, that little devil would go in th living room an shut that do' between th kitchen an th living room an shut hisself up in there. He would sit down on th flo'. When I get ready t feed him I couldnt find him. I'd say,

DANCER

"Where that little devil at?"

NARRATOR

I go in there an find him an he'd act as if he didnt want t be in there where I was. I'd say,

DANCER

"Get up from there, boy. Get in here an eat this food."

NARRATOR

He'd get up. When his mama come home I'd tell her what he did an she said,

SINGER

"Clydie, let me tell you something—ignore him. If you fix him somethin' t eat an he dont eat, dont worry about it. An you do your work. All I ask is that you keep th do's closed so he dont go walkin' out th house."

NARRATOR

When I quit foolin' wit him, every time I turned around he had a hol' a me. He was scared a me at first, I walk near him an he'd holler like I was a panther or somethin'. That boy tickled me 'cause he was scared of me. He'd never seen a nigger before but, hell, I was near 'bout white as he was. Or maybe it was 'cause they had never had nobody in th house before. They never had had a maid. They come from North Carolina t Emory. Then he grew outta it an I couldnt get way from him. I was sorry when he got outta it 'cause every time I turn around he was right behind me. Most doctors in Emory worked in th home an they paid good money. I'd work a day. Some of them I'd work two days. I'd do my five days. I did that for a long time. I likeded that. I didnt like t do nothin' but day work. I liked t go different places. Back in them days you made more money with day work. There werent too many black people workin' in these big stores an th only work you had was something like this. I did that work for a long time.
. . .

number 23

> (*Dancer takes a laundry basket full of soiled, white baby clothes over to the washing machine and begins washing. She goes about the task with obvious pleasure.*)

DANCER

It's amazing how much dirty laundry a newborn can produce in just two weeks. Th hamper's overflowing with cloth diapers, swaddling blankets, bibs, sleepers, knit caps, nursing bras, an onesies.

Clydie th Great taught my mother an mama taught me. Some clothes go in th dryer. Others hang on th line. On days when th sky is clear, th sun is better than bleach. But you cant hang clothes on a line any ol' way 'cause they wont dry right. Most people these days dont know that. An they dont know that theres a difference between Tide an Ivory Snow. For th baby, a shiny new baby, nothing beats getting whites white better than Ivory Snow an sunshine.

Mama taught me t fill th washing machine tub with water before putting in th garments. She used laundry powder that dissolved better in a full tub of water. But I got liquid detergent, so I can skip that step. Just measure th detergent an pour it into th dispenser. My new machine—brought in honor of my newborn baby. Set it t hot wash/cold rinse. Push start.

*(The sound of water filling the washing machine
an clothes washing. Machine sounds. Later, Dancer
returns to take clean clothes out of the washer.)*

DANCER

What in th world!

(The onesies come out of the machine the color of rust. Sobbing.)

Th baby's clothes are ruined!

SINGER

(singing)

All day long I'm slaving; all day long I'm busting suds.
All day long I'm slaving; all day long I'm busting suds.
Keep my hands a tired, washing out these dirty duds.

Lord I do more work than forty 'leven gold dust twins.
Lord I do more work than forty 'leven gold dust twins.
Got myself a achin' from head down t my shins.

Sorry I do washing just t make my livelihood.
Sorry I do washing just t make my livelihood.
Although washwoman's life it aint a bit a good.

Rather be a scullion cooking in some white folks yard.
Rather be a scullion cooking in some white folks yard.
I could eat a plenty, wouldnt have t work so hard.

Me an my old washboard, sure do have some cares an woes.
Me an my old washboard, sure do have some cares an woes.
In th muddy water, wringing out these dirty clothes.

NARRATOR

number 24

SINGER

Th old folks used t call blues devil music. They were clear about such things. So clear. They waded out in slack water like John th Baptist. Or they stood witness along th bank. They went down in th water, quiet except for th singing, of course, an rose with a powerful testimony:

DANCER

"These are they which came out of th great tribulation, an have washed their robes, an made them white in th blood of th Lamb." —Revelations 7:14

NARRATOR

number 25

. . .

How t Remove Blood Stains from Panties

Whats needed: hydrogen peroxide
Dove soap
dish detergent
cold running water
sink
panties stained with blood

SINGER

Periods arent easy t contain.

DANCER

Even with th extra protection offered by Always with "wings,"

SINGER

panties often get soiled.

NARRATOR

Th edges, where th elastic is sewn into th fabric with those zigzag stitches, are th most likely t stain. Th ridges draw th blood into th seams. So it's particularly important that these areas receive careful attention as soon as you take th panties off. In order t prevent stains in delicate undergarments, every menstruating woman should keep a bottle of hydrogen peroxide in th vanity beneath th bathroom sink. Not only does hydrogen peroxide kill germs in minor scrapes an cuts, but it is effective at removing organic stains from fabric. In order t apply th peroxide effectively, create a well, cotton side up in th area of th stain so that when you pour th peroxide it puddles in th well. Th peroxide will not be absorbed immediately into th fabric so hold th pool carefully t give it time t react t th blood. Th peroxide will bubble an turn into white foam wherever th blood has stained. Hold a bar of Dove under cold water for a moment, then rub th wet bar over th soiled areas. After saturating th areas of concern with Dove, grab th panties firmly in your fists, with th soiled areas between your thumb an forefingers. Rub th soiled areas together briskly back an forth for a moment before continuing th motion under a steady stream of cold running water. Do not allow th water t flow too quickly because it will wash away th cleansing agents before th stains are removed from th fabric. Continue rubbing in like manner until all th stains are removed. Rinse thoroughly. Stop th drain an fill th sink with cold water. Then apply a small amount of dish detergent or delicate cycle laundry detergent t th panties. Dip th panties into th water an pull back out of th water. Trap a pocket of air into a balloon of wet fabric. Slowly squeeze th air through th fabric. This process forces detergent through th pores of th fabric. Repeat until th garment has been carefully cleaned. Drain th sink. Rinse panties with cool water until they feel free of th slipperiness of soap. Hang th panties over th shower rod until dry.

. . .

number 26

. . .

A Move in th Right Direction

We learn that at th next meeting of th city council, an ordinance will be offered requiring all washerwomen belonging t any "association" or "society" t pay a business tax or license.

We also learn that th new steam laundry company will apply for exemption from city taxation for ten years, an trust that our city fathers will grant their petition unanimously. Th new steam laundry company will necessarily be at large expense for th first year or two, but as their business will greatly inure t th benefit of at least nine tenths of our population, our council should not overlook its importance.

—*Atlanta Constitution*, July 26, 1881

. . .

number 27

DANCER

From a small headline "Th Washerwomen Strike" on th last page of th Thursday, July 21, 1881, edition t front-page news of Friday, July 29, 1881, in th *Atlanta Constitution*:

NARRATOR

TH WET CLOTHES TH WASHERWOMEN BRING HOME.

Th Story of th Organization Fully Told by Captain Starnes, Who Says a White Man an Three Hundred Dollars Back th Strikers—Th Way th Banks Are Increased.

SINGER

Police court was well attended yesterday morning, an Recorder Glenn added one hundred an thirty-five dollars t th city treasury by fines imposed.

Among other cases disposed of were those against Matilda Crawford, Sallie Bell, Carrie Jones, Dora Jones, Orphelia Turner an Sarah A. Collier. Th sixtette of ebony hued damsels was charged with disorderly conduct an quarreling, an in each case, except th last, a fine of five dollars was imposed, an subsequently paid. In th case of Sarah A. Collier, twenty dollars was assessed, an th money not being paid, th defendant's name was transcribed t th chain-gang book, where it will remain for forty days.

Each of these cases resulted from th washerwomen's strike. As members of th organization they have visited women who are taking no part in th strike an have threatened personal violence unless their demands were acceded t an their example followed. During their rounds they met with persons who opposed th strike an who declined t submit t their proposition t become members. This opposition caused an excessive use of abusive an threatening language an th charge of disorderly conduct an quarreling was th result.

Soon after court, a CONSTITUTION representative heard Captain Starnes remark,

DANCER

"Well, Glenn's a good one; he put th fine on th strikers an tomorrow we will have additional subjects for his consideration."

SINGER

This remark caused th reporter t ask Starnes if he knew what he was talking about.

DANCER

"Of course I do. Bagby an I have been working on this matter ever since th strike began, an if anybody in town knows anything about, I guess we do."

NARRATOR

"Well, tell us what you know."

DANCER

"Well, you see this society was first organized about one year ago. Th first meeting was held in a church on Summer Hill, but only a few women attended. They tried hard t get up a strike but could not succeed an th thing soon broke because no one would join. This year however, they have been successful an t-day nearly three thousand negro women are making their white friends who supported them during th cold, hard winter t pay them a dollar a dozen for washing."

NARRATOR

"You say they organized a year ago!"

DANCER

"Yes, but that organization went t pieces. Th society that now exists is about two weeks old. Next Saturday night three weeks ago twenty negro women an a few negro men met in Summer Hill church an discussed th matter. Th next night th negro preachers in all th churches announced a mass meeting of th washerwomen for th following night at Summer Hill church. Th meeting was a big one an th result was an organization. Officers were elected, committees appointed an time an places for meeting read out. Since then there has been meetings every night or two, an now there is a club or society in every ward in th city an th strikers have increased from twenty t about three thousand in less than three weeks."

NARRATOR

"What do they do at these meetings?"

DANCER

"Make speeches an pray. They swear they never will wash another piece for less than one dollar a dozen, but they will never get it an will soon give in. In fact, they would have caved before this but for th white man who is backing th strike."

NARRATOR

"Do you know that there is a white man behind these strikers, or is it a rumor?"

DANCER

"I know it, an I'll tell you who it is if you want t know."

NARRATOR

"No, never mind his name. Tell me how you know."

DANCER

"I have heard it from several responsible parties. There is Dora Watts, who lives at Mr. Wolfe's, 144 Jones Street, who swears that a white man addressed a meeting last week. She also says that he will speak t them next Monday night. This man tells them that he will see them through all right. They have a fund of three hundred dollars an feel confident of getting what they ask."

NARRATOR

"They are trying t prevent those who are not members from washing, are they not?"

DANCER

"Yes. Th committee first goes t those who have no connection with th organization an try t persuade them t join. Failing in this they notify them that they must not take any more washing at less than one dollar a dozen, an then threaten them with cowhides, fire an death if they disobey. Out on Walker Street there lives a white lady, a Mrs. Richardson, who has had but one washerwoman for eight years. Her name is Sarah Gardner. Her husband joined th strikers an would not let his wife take th washing. Mrs. Richardson hired another woman who took her clothes away Monday but brought them back in th afternoon saying that th 'committee wouldnt let her wash for less than a dollar a dozen.' Mrs. Richardson then induced a girl she had in th house t undertake th washing but yesterday evening while she was at work on Mrs. Richardson's place, a committee composed of Dora Shorter, Annie King an Sam Gardner came up an threatened t kill her if she didnt stop, an when th lady, Mrs. Richardson, came out an ordered them away, they refused t go, an began t abuse her. I heard of it an now all three are here, an Spyers has th key. He is fond of locking, but hates t unlock a door. I guess Recorder Glenn will catch 'em for twenty dollars each."

NARRATOR

"So they are on their muscle?"

DANCER

"Well, I should say so. Th men are as bad as th women. When a woman refuses t join th society, their men threaten t 'whip 'em,' an th result is that th ranks are daily swelling. Why, last night there was a big meeting at New Hope church, on Green's Ferry Street, an fifty additions were made t th list. They passed resolutions informing all women not members of th society t quit work, or stand th consequences. I tell you, this strike is a big thing, but if Glenn will only stand t Bagby an myself we will break it up. I am going t arrest every one who threatens any woman, an I am going t try t get th chain gang full, then they will stop. Why, let me tell you, out here on Spring Street is an old white woman who lives over her wash tub. Th infernal scoundrels went t her house yesterday an threatened t burn th place down an t kill her if she took another rag. Emma Palmer, Jane Webb an Sarah Collier, with two white women, are doing th work, but I think Spyers will get a chance t lock 'em up before dark."

—*Atlanta Constitution*, July 26, 1881

(*Dancer dancing. Music. RHYTHM SECTION.*)

NARRATOR

number 28

SINGER

Th Igbo, coming from th west coast of Africa in th region now known as Nigeria, held stubborn beliefs. For instance, once disembarked from th slave ship, still in chains, Igbo have been known t walk not westward up th banks of th Georgia coastal islands but eastward into th seas. Singing in their native tongue: Th water brought us, th water will take us away.

NARRATOR

(*singing the call as others join in response,
to the tune "Won't Dat Be a Time"*)

Oh, wont dat be a mighty time
   Wont dat be a time
Yeah, won't dat be a mighty time
   Wont dat be a time

Werent dat water dat brought us here
   De water brought us here
Werent dat water dat brought us here
   De water brought us here
Wont da water then take us away
   De water will take us away
Gone let dat north wind blow on me
   Wont dat be a time
Come 'long brother an play your drum
   Wont dat be a time
Oh eatin' of th fish an drinkin' of th wine
   Wont dat be a time
If water brought us here
   Water will take us away

. . .

number 29

(Narrator steps up on chair soapbox.)

Mr. Jim English, Mayor of Atlanta
Atlanta, Georgia, August 1, 1881

Dear Sir:
We th members of our society are determined t stand t our pledge an make extra charges for washing, an we have agreed, an are willing t pay twenty-five dollars or fifty dollars for licenses as a protection, so we can control th washing for th city. We can afford t pay these licenses, an will do it before we will be defeated, an then we will have full control of th city's washing at our own prices, as th city has control of our husbands' work at their prices. Dont forget this. We hope t hear from your council Tuesday morning. We mean business this week or no washing.

Yours respectfully,

From five Societies, four hundred an eighty-six Members
   —*Atlanta Constitution*, August 3, 1881

(Narrator steps down from chair soapbox.)

. . .

number 30

SINGER

She did laundry every day but Sunday. Clothes hanging on a line. Outside most of th year; but inside sometimes. Aunti Queen fussing,

NARRATOR

"Aunt Clydie, you dont have t do laundry every day."

SINGER

Clydie th Great never paid her any mind. She kept about her chores, washing, quilting, an crocheting blankets out of yarn. One time, when I was a girl, she asked me t put a lit match t th end of yarn. She would burn th ends of th thread so that th crochet would not unravel. But her grip was weakened by arthritis. So she asked me t light th match. Then one end of yarn was too long, an when I lit it, it winced an whipped around, still burning, an melted quickly on her forefinger. I was mortified. But she expressed less emotion than th thread. She—th injured—soothing me—th uninjured—instead of th other way around.

I saw then, for th first time, th locked chest wherein she kept her treasures.

DANCER

"It has t hurt."

NARRATOR

"Be still child. Jus be still."

SINGER

Then there was this other time. Late, very late, almost at th end. She an I were together in th kitchen. I was eating at th table. She just finished an taking her plate t th sink when suddenly, unexpectedly she lost control of her bowels—spilling through her clothes an onto th floor. I was paralyzed. Calcified. Sliced as if from a motion picture reel an discarded on th editing room floor.

I wish I remembered helping her t undress. If only I could remember taking her soiled clothes from her an wrapping her in a towel. Taking her into a warm tub an sponging her in lavender water. Wrapping her in terry cloth an rubbing coconut oil on her feet, her legs, her back. Opening th drawer an setting a pile of fresh things t wear beside her on th bed.

An I'd like t recall th strong smell of Pine-Sol an rubber gloves as I poured brown water down th washroom sink. If I only had th faintest recollection of scalding my hand while holding her panties under hot running water—as I know she had done for me.

. . .

Then th water would have washed away my shame.

(*Dancer dancing. Music. FAST FLUTE SOLO.*)

NARRATOR

number 31

. . .

On those Sundays, while standing at th river's edge, th congregation would sing. Th water pacing out now, revealing what it had hidden twelve hours ago beneath its skirts. Th people call after her. An they follow out from th edge.

Th water has been here since th beginning.

SINGER

(*singing*)

Take me t th water—

NARRATOR

Washing.

SINGER

(*singing*)

Take me t th water—

NARRATOR

Remembering.

SINGER

(*singing*)

Take me t th water—
T be baptized.

ALL

(*singing*)

Take me t th water—
Take me t th water—
Take me t th water—
T be baptized.

(*Blackout*)
END OF PLAY

ROUTES

(after "Seventh Street" in Cane *by Jean Toomer)*

Money burns th pocket, pocket hurts,
Hustlers dealing in Gucci shirts,
Whip, souped-up Cadillac,
Cruising, cruising 'bove th subway tracks.

U Street is a bastard of red lining an th war on drugs. A crude-boned, soft-skinned wedge of ghetto life breathing this triflin air, Go Go an love, thrusting unconscious rhythms, black reddish blood into th white an whitewashed ground of DC. Stale soggy ground of th Chocolate City. Fences lean in soggy ground . . . Brace it! Tap it! Again! Right it! . . . th sun. Chain-link fence posts are brilliant in th sun; braids of fence mesh rust an break away. Black reddish blood. Pouring for crude-boned soft-skinned life, who set you flowing? Blood suckers of th street head would be spinning if they drank your blood. Gentrification would put a stop t it. Who set you flowing? White an whitewash disappear in blood. Who set you flowing? Flowing down th smooth asphalt of U Street, in row houses, brick office buildings, theaters, corner stores, carryouts, an clubs? Standin on th corners? Swirling like a blood-red smoke up where th buzzards fly in heaven? God would not dare t suck black red blood. A black God! He would duck his head in shame an call for th Judgment Day. Who set you flowing?

Money burns th pocket, pocket hurts,
Hustlers dealing in Gucci shirts,
Whip, souped-up Cadillac,
Cruising, cruising 'bove th subway tracks.

EMPTY VESSEL

(in three pieces)

i

On th morning of my birthday I awoke with clear memories of my grandmother brightening my mind. She was bent, inspecting th patch of garden my father planted behind th house. Wearing her green sweater an a pair of elastic-waist polyester pants, her white hair parted down th middle an braided in two cornrows. Her wide brimmed bifocals firmly on her face—characteristically quiet. Busy. Working as she did in solitude. So much of her day was spent that way, toiling quietly at some task.

I know what my grandmother did t earn her living because of th ways she served our family. I didnt learn it through stories she told or things scribbled on a page. She didnt write very well—after th strokes, she was left-handed an she always wrote her *N*'s backwards. An she was quiet, but not because of th strokes. She was quiet because she didnt trust too many words. Or people who used them. My childhood was peppered with her warnings against those people whom someone in my family would bring home who "ran their mouth too much." If they told all their business, they'd show no respect for yours. Dont talk. Keep quiet. An do until you cant.

My father was from th country too. He tended t keep a garden in th yard. Nearly every year found my father honoring th season: tilling, planting, watering, harvesting. Rotating th crops. I dont recall a time when my grandmother asked for a particular planting, preferring one over another. It was my father's garden. But she always worked it. She tended th tomatoes. Pulled th collards. She picked th pole beans that were strung in th row nearest th garage—a diminutive figure among th poles, strings, beans, an other things growing so well under her careful hand. Th squash could take over or th eggplant, but my grandmother knew how t tend them.

Th image of her that arose so vividly in my mind this morning reminded me that I have no memory of her ever speaking about her work. I know th work that she performed in her youth because of what she chose in her twilight. She sewed incessantly. I have quilts she made from scraps of my childhood memories: curtains, bedding, dresses, shirts, jeans, all kinds of discarded things. She crocheted hundreds of skeins of yarn into blankets for our bedding. She didnt knit—th strokes took th use of her good hand. She washed dishes but she rarely cooked. She split th logs my father brought home by th truckload an heaped in th backyard. My brothers would help him line th logs in rows along th fence. An a little at a time th logs were split into quarters or thirds or halves by one of them: one of my brothers, sometimes my father, but often my grandmother. Sometimes I would pile a few logs in th wheelbarrow an bring them into th house, but I never split logs. I tried but my grandmother could do things with an axe that I never learned how t do. An while she taught me a lot about sewing, she didnt teach me how t swing an axe.

ii

She was born in 1908 or 1906; we dont really know which. It might have mattered tremendously t a schoolgirl, but th difference is negligible at this point. If she were here now she'd tell you that she was, in fact, born. A fact that prevails in spite of th capriciousness of documented history. An if th year matters, it is on a timeline like th one Pilate cites in Toni Morrison's novel *Song of Solomon*—it was th year they elected William Howard Taft; th year they had that race riot in Springfield, Illinois, that prompted th formation of th NAACP. She was born in Jasper County, Georgia, just two generations removed from th Emancipation Proclamation, at th time when Jim Crow had stretched his unruly wings an roosted himself firmly in th branch of every southern tree.

Jim Crow had become th Law, an th Law is a tool of conquest. An until those sitting in th duly designated national seats of power became uncomfortable enough t disengage th scavenger, Jim Crow wielded th force necessary t clarify facts th Law seemed t confuse—such as just whom th Founding Fathers meant in their founding documents t possess these inalienable rights. But for black folk, like my grandmother, neither white people's use of force nor their words were clarifying. Grandma knew that th Law was th way that white people struggled t keep control over things they did not have control over. She also knew that what folks said had little t do with what they actually did. Language could be treacherous, an in th same way that it held no allegiance t one's actions, it did not belong t her either. For my grandmother, language had its benefits but silence was more useful.

iii

When she died, I was seventeen. We buried her on Thanksgiving Day. My godmother sang "I'll Fly Away," an her voice lifted my mother in her grief. I remember th heights of that song. An I remember th funny double shadow created by two bright lights shining behind me on either side, which made my neck appear on th pew in front of me as abnormally thin while my head seemed gigantic. Hazy, inadequate memories.

However, I recall more clearly th day I was sent t bring my grandmother home. She had been staying with my cousin Evelyn, who lived at Eighth an E Streets in Northeast Washington, DC—a few blocks from Union Station on Capitol Hill. I rarely ventured into two of th three stories in th row house where she lived. Instead, on our frequent trips t my cousin's house, my family descended three steep concrete steps, which fell beneath th more inviting wrought iron stairs leading t th formal first-floor entry, an entered th home through th basement. Th old storm door whined an fought as if defending th residence from trespassers. Th second floor was guarded by a framed picture of th holy trinity—Jesus, John F. Kennedy, an Martin Luther King. They kept vigil over rooms of pretentious furniture, dressed like women hiding gray hair beneath black wigs an veiled hats. Th uppermost floor was peopled by an ever-changing array of strange old men. Neither floor alluring.

When my grandmother visited, she served as th caregiver for her niece, whose hard living an ill temperament rendered her less able. But my cousin called this time t ask my mother t cut my grandmother's visit short. "Aunt Neek," which is what Cousin Evelyn called my grandmother, "is acting funny." So my mother sent me t get her. I had managed t get her home an into th house. But my father picked her up gingerly in his arms an carried her t th car t take her t th hospital.

She'd had another stroke. Th doctors scanned her brain, but they werent able t distinguish th recent damage from that done by th strokes decades earlier. So they relied on a battery of tests t gather information. I cant remember how long she had been in an out of th hospital, but on this occasion she had been getting better. Grandma was sitting up in bed crocheting another blanket when a long white lab coat accented by th obligatory stethoscope entered followed by a shorter white lab coat also draping one who might have been th other's son. In a couple of decades there would be no difference between th salt-an-pepper authority that distinguished th one with th horn-rimmed glasses from th one with th hungry, green eyes. Th green eyes studying th horn-rimmed glasses as he held up a series of pictures of common items an asked my grandmother, "Can you identify this?"

My grandmother was unimpressed by th lab coat, th horn-rimmed glasses, th stethoscope, his picture cards, or th hungry, green eyes. She continued crocheting. Th younger scribbled notes on a chart while th elder continued asking my grandmother questions about th pictures. He moved through a few cards before th doctors excused themselves upon th behest of a nurse. In th opening left by their absence, I cajoled my grandmother. "Grandma, cant you just answer their questions?" She continued crocheting. When th doctors returned, th older doctor smiled, offered a friendly explanation for their departure, an then resumed with th cards. This time it was a picture of a spoon. "Can you tell me what this is?"

Finally, Grandma responded. She put down her hook an looked at th doctor. "Do you know what that is?"

He nodded an replied, "Yes."

"Well good." She nodded. Grandma picked up her crochet hook an yarn an went back t work. Tha's real good.

PRAYER

(after "Prayer" from Cane *by Jean Toomer)*

My body is opaque t th soul.
    not black   not blue   not white like you
    have yearned t be

Driven of th spirit, long have I sought t temper it unto th spirit's
    longing,
But my mind, too, is opaque t th soul.
    not yellow   not red   not redbone nor
    high yellow

A closed lid is my soul's flesh-eye.
O Spirits of whom my soul is but a little finger,
Direct it t th lid of its flesh-eye.
    not brown

I am weak with much giving.
    whats blessed is blessed   an cannot
    be otherwise

I am weak with th desire t give more.
    green   verdant   an fecund

(How strong a thing is th little finger!)
So weak that I have confused th body with th soul,
An th body with its little finger.
(How frail is th little finger.)

    whats green is strong   an cannot
    be otherwise

My voice could not carry t you did you dwell in stars,
O Spirits of whom my soul is but a little finger.

Acknowledgments

The author would like to thank the editors of the following publications for first publishing these selections (sometimes in different versions):

"Rhobert" in *Aunt Chloe: A Journal of Artful Candor*
Period. in *Aunt Chloe: A Journal of Artful Candor*
"*Amita*" in *The Other Anthology Not White/Straight/Male/Healthy Enough: Being "Other" in the Academy*
"June" in *The Masters Review Anthology*
"Empty Vessel" in *New Writing: The International Journal for the Practice and Theory of Creative Writing*
Waterbearers in *Wayne State Literary Review*
"Won't Dat Be a Time." John and Ruby Lomax 1939 Southern States Recording Trip (AFC 1939/001). American Folklife Center, Library of Congress.

About the Author

V **Efua Prince** is a professor of African American studies at Wayne State University, who specializes in themes of home, women, and housework. She has previously served as a W.E.B. Du Bois Fellow at Harvard University; a visiting scholar at the Carter G. Woodson Institute, University of Virginia; and Avalon Professor of Humanities at Hampton University. Her first book, *Burnin' Down the House: Home in African American Literature*, was recognized by Academia as a university press bestseller.